Outlaw

Blain Larkin and his brother Moylan run afoul of Verne Lecroy, son of a powerful banker. When Lecroy kills Moylan in a gunfight Blain tries to revenge his brother's death but only manages to wound Lecroy. The youngster is sentenced to hang for attempted murder.

Blain goes on the run, and in order to survive joins an outlaw gang led by Robert Sturdy. Blain is resigned to the life of an owlhoot, but when he meets Sturdy's sister, the delightful Emelie, he resolves to lead a better life. That ain't gonna happen any time soon as the youngster battles to survive treachery within the outlaw gang, and the vengefulness of Verne Lecroy.

Outlaw

Philip McCormac

A Black Horse Western

ROBERT HALE

© Philip McCormac 2020
First published in Great Britain 2020

ISBN 978-0-7198-3089-1

The Crowood Press
The Stable Block
Crowood Lane
Ramsbury
Marlborough
Wiltshire SN8 2HR

www.bhwesterns.com

Robert Hale is an imprint
of The Crowood Press

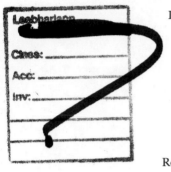

Typeset by
Derek Doyle & Associates, Shaw Heath
Printed and bound in Great Britain by
4Bind Ltd, Stevenage, SG1 2XT

1

Blain Larkin awoke with a start to the sound of someone screaming. For bewildered moments he wondered where he was. There was a flurry of movement beside him and he turned to see his naked companion struggling into a wrap.

'Agatha,' he began, then stopped.

Agatha was using cuss words even he would have been ashamed to use. Blain had never heard such language from a woman. Still mouthing profanities she dashed from the room.

Muddleheaded, he sat up in the bed. Last night he and his brother Moylan had ridden into Callender, having been paid off after the cattle drive. Like most cowboys they had drunk some, and then decided to take in the delights of the local cathouse. Now Blain had been rudely awakened by some row taking place inside the bordello.

'Damn!' he muttered 'Sounds like some poor gal's being murdered.'

The screaming went on and on and on. Someone in mortal terror or in terrible pain. People were shouting. Doors were banging. Footsteps pounded on stairs and corridors.

Blain's head was aching. His throat was dry and he had a foul taste in his mouth. Not knowing what else to do, he threw off the bedcovers and slid his feet on to the floor.

The youngster groped around in the semidarkness for his

5

clothes. The riotous noise was ongoing. He found his trousers and pulled them on. Not bothering with a shirt he went out into the corridor. A scene of confusion met his gaze. Men and women in various stages of undress were milling about on the passageway and stairs. Some held candles or lamps aloft.

The noise was concentrated down the bottom end of the corridor. Blain forced a passage through the swarm of people. At last he caught sight of Agatha, the woman he had spent the night with. She was pounding on a door and yelling at someone inside.

'Open this blasted door! What the hell's going on in there? I've sent for the sheriff. He'll be here any minute. Come on, open up!'

As she shouted and cursed she slapped the flat of her hand against the door.

'Help me! Help me!' a shrill voice called from inside the room.

A man pushed roughly past Blain. He was about to remonstrate with him, and then saw it was his brother, Moylan.

'What on earth's going on?' Moylan called.

Like Blain, Moylan was dressed only in his pants. He had powerful arms and shoulders. In the dim light his torso bulged heavy with muscle. He reached Agatha and took hold of her shoulder.

'What is it? What's going on?'

'It's my girl in there. That's Lecroy in there, murdering her.' She turned from Moylan and yelled through the door. 'Dessie, are you all right?'

'Help me, Agatha, please help me!' came the pathetic reply. 'Oh, dear God, help!'

A man's voice could be heard shouting drunkenly.

'You goddamned whore, I'll teach you!'

There was a sound of bare flesh being slapped. The girl's screams grew even more desperate.

6

'Stand back.'

Moylan pushed the distraught madam from the door. He was being firm but gentle as he steered Agatha to one side. Blain pressed forward, wanting to be near his brother whatever happened.

'Lecroy, you heathen!' Moylan yelled. 'Open this door afore I'm forced to break it down, you blackguard.'

After this ultimatum there was silence from inside the room. There came the sound of a gunshot and a ball smashed a hole through the panel of the door, only just missing Moylan. Moylan immediately flung himself to one side. His eyes were wide with anger as he stared at the bullet hole in the door.

'Goddamn you, Lecroy, what the hell you playing at? That goddamn shot nearly took my head off!'

'Stay there, fella, and I'll try again to put a hole in your hide.'

The gun blasted out as the door panel was shot to pieces. Moylan's eyes were wide with anger. Then to Blain's consternation his brother stepped up to the door once more, raised his leg and kicked his heel against it. There was a rending of wood as the door splintered around the lock. Moylan threw himself bodily against it, then everything gave way and Moylan plunged through the opening.

'Moylan!' Blain called, suddenly realizing what his brother was up to.

Moylan was hoping to get inside and disarm the madman before he managed to reload. Blain, mindless of his own danger, rushed into the room after his brother.

Once inside he could see Moylan had read the situation right. He was fighting with a tall, well-built man over possession of a pistol. The combatants were fairly matched in strength as they grunted and strained for possession of the weapon. Then Blain noticed the girl. His eyes widened.

She was lying on the bed face down, her back and buttocks covered in blood and her hands bound to the bedposts. She was craning her head around in an effort to see what was going on. Blain was torn between going to the aid of his brother and helping the girl.

Moylan jerked his head forwards, smashing it against his opponent's nose. The man cursed and pulled back, blood streaming from his busted nose. Moylan hooked his foot around his opponent's leg and heaved. They both went down with Moylan on top. Lecroy was still gripping the pistol and Moylan banged his hand against the floor. The grip loosened and the pistol dropped away.

The cowboy battered his opponent. Moylan had the advantage of being on top and was punishing Lecroy with both fists. Agatha rushed past Blain.

'Oh Dessie, my poor girl.'

Agatha fumbled at the bindings, and Blain moved to help her. Moylan left off hitting his opponent and clambered to his feet, leaving Lecroy with a bruised and bloodied face. The injured man was groaning and swearing at the same time.

'I'm gonna kill you, you son of a bitch,' Lecroy gritted.

Moylan grabbed up the discarded pistol and aimed it at the man on the floor.

'Not if I kill you first.'

As he spoke, two men pushed inside the room.

'Verne, what the hell's going on?'

The speaker was in his twenties, of pale complexion with wide-spaced, bulging eyes and a bushy moustache. His companion was much older, with regular, well-defined features. He had a narrow face and a wiry build.

'Auther, these fellows burst in and attacked me. Kill the sons of bitches!'

The younger man turned to Moylan and took a step towards him. His companion moved to back him up. Moylan aimed the gun he had taken from Lecroy.

'You fellows want to tackle me, you'll have to argue with this pistol. I advise you to take Lecroy here and remove him from these premises pronto. I'm hard put not to put a bullet in him. A man who does that to a female ain't no man at all.'

The men looked from Moylan, to the injured girl. Agatha stood helplessly looking down at her ruined back.

'What did he do that for?' she lamented. 'Why was he cutting the poor girl?'

It was Blain who spotted the riding crop on the floor. He picked it up.

'He was using this on her.'

'Jeez!' Moylan swore. 'If you men hold him I'll try that whip out on him. See how he likes a taste of rawhide.'

'You won't touch him! You don't know who you're messing with. That's Verne Lecroy, Mortimer Lecroy's son. You're already in deep trouble for attacking him.'

'I'm in trouble? It was that coyote as was beating this poor gal. If his pa is any sort'a man he'd take that whip and tan his hide.'

Lecroy rolled on to his knees and clambered to his feet. He wiped his hand across his face and stared at the blood on his fingers.

'I want satisfaction, you sheep-dip. No one, but no one hits Verne Lecroy and gets away with it.'

Moylan held the pistol steady on the three men as they stared balefully back at him.

'Lecroy, it's taking me all my self-control not to pull this trigger and blow you to kingdom come. You're nothing but the scrapings from the gutter. A man as beats a woman doesn't deserve to live. You're not a man at all, but a cowardly dog. You're brave enough beating helpless gals. You didn't do too well against me when I came in here and took your gun away.'

Verne Lecroy's bloody and bruised face twisted up with hatred as he stared at the man taunting him.

'I want satisfaction,' he gritted through clenched teeth. 'Are you afraid to meet me man to man?'

'Afraid? Huh! I'll give you satisfaction, all right. I'll beat the living daylights outta you, you snivelling cur.'

Lecroy's lip curled with distain.

'Not fists, you uncouth pig. I mean guns. Out in the street. A good old-fashioned shoot-out. Are you man enough for that?'

Moylan stared incredulously at the speaker.

'A shoot-out! Are you talking about a shoot-out – a gun-fight?'

'Frightened, eh!' Lecroy sneered. 'You're brave enough holding a gun on us. What if one of us pulled a pistol and started firing at you? How brave are you then? I'm challeng-ing you to a duel. Man to man. Or are you too cowardly for such a confrontation? It takes a real man to take part in a gun-fight!'

The three men glowered at Moylan. His eyes flicked from face to face.

'Is he serious?' he asked.

'Of course he's serious. If you want to chicken out, we'll understand. Just curl your tail between your legs, apologize and slink away. At least that way you might live to enjoy another night in this bordello.'

'Damn you! You think I'm afraid of this piece of horse dung? I accept your challenge. Name the place and time and I'll be there.'

There was a gleam of triumph in Lecroy's eyes.

'I look forward to our meeting; that is, if you don't turn tail and run.'

'I'll be there, damn you. You'll regret crossing swords with Moylan Larkin!'

Lecroy grabbed up a bundle of clothes, saying 'Now, if you'll excuse me, I'll pull my drawers on and leave you.' Then he stalked from the room, followed by his two companions.

2

'Moylan, you can't take up this challenge.' Agatha rinsed a piece of bloodied cotton in water before continuing. 'Lecroy has been in gunfights in the past. I know of at least three men he has severely wounded or killed.'

They had brought towels and basins of hot water to the injured girl and were tending her wounds. As they worked she moaned quietly. Her back was a mess of lacerations where the leather had cut into soft flesh.

'Goddamn, Agatha, you think I'm afraid of that piece of horseshit! I'll put a bullet in his guts and he'll never beat another female again.'

'Please Moylan, take my advice. Even if by some stroke of good luck you do wound or hurt Lecroy, his father will hound you to death. He more or less owns this town. He has power of life or death over us all. If you hurt his son he would leave no stone unturned to bring you to the gallows or have you killed. These people have no morals. They have no sense of right and wrong. They bribe and cheat their way into power and then rule with a rod of iron. It wouldn't surprise me if the sheriff don't arrive in the morning and demand me to shut down. I pay a bribe for them to leave me alone. At anytime they can increase the bite and I have to pay up or cease plying my trade.'

'You mean you pay those jackals so you can keep your business running?' Moylan sounded incredulous. 'What sort of game is that?'

'Moylan, wise up, this is the real world. Look at poor Dessie here. She has no redress against the likes of Lecroy. If she goes to the sheriff he'll more than likely toss her in jail.'

'Well, that settles it then, the sooner someone puts a bullet in Lecroy, the better.'

'Men and their stupid pride!' Agatha snapped.

Her gaze fell on Blain who was doing his best to swab the blood from Dessie's ruined back. Her eyes softened.

'I'm sorry. It's been such a strange night. You save my girl from a savage beating and all I do is rant at you. Just promise me one thing. If you must go through with this stupid gunfight, keep Blain out of it.'

After she spoke these words, Agatha left the room and Moylan followed. Blain could hear them continuing the discussion outside.

As Blain bathed the lacerated flesh he guessed the young woman was not much older than himself. He had never thought about the realities of life in a brothel. In fact he knew nothing about the trade. Men came here and bought the favours of the women. Once they purchased those favours, it appeared they could do what they liked with them. Up until then the excitement of the illicit sex had blinded him to the grim realities of prostitution. Now he was dealing with the harsh truth of it.

Even as he pondered these facts the girl turned her head and gazed at him. She had a soft, round face somewhat swollen from weeping. Her hair was a tangled mass of dark curls. She smiled at him through her tears.

'I saw you come in tonight. Agatha took a real shine to you. I don't blame her. I can't think of many men who would bother helping a girl like me.'

Blain blushed and smiled at her.

'You must be very sore,' he said.

'It hurts like hell. I'd like to do the same to that bastard Lecroy.'

Blain was shocked by the girl's language. He was saved further embarrassment by the return of Agatha. She was carrying a jar of salve.

'Go down the kitchen and grab some breakfast,' she told him. 'Tomas is there with Moylan. I'll join you as soon as I've finished here.'

Blain stood up and stretched. Suddenly he realized how hungry he was. His belly grumbled loudly, and he looked sheepishly at the woman as he rubbed the offending organ. Agatha with sudden fondness pulled him close.

'You are a good man, Blain,' she murmured in his ear. 'I hope you'll come again and see me.'

'You bet,' he said earnestly. 'I'll visit as often as I can.'

There was something wistful in the madam's eyes as she released him and pushed him towards the door.

'Go on now and get some breakfast,' she urged.

Blain joined Moylan at the kitchen table where they tucked into generous portions of eggs and bacon. Before they left they promised to visit again soon.

'Are you really going through with this duel business?' Blain asked Moylan as they made their way into town.

'I reckon so, Blain. Would you have any respect for me if I chickened out?'

'It wouldn't change a thing. You're my brother.'

'Blain, you are so innocent. No wonder the girls in the brothel fell for you.'

'Girls – there was only one – Agatha.' Blain's eyes glazed over slightly as he recalled the exploits of the night. 'She invited me to visit her again.'

Moylan regarded his younger brother with an amused grin.

'Can I tell you, Blain, there wasn't a girl there that wouldn't gladly have taken Agatha's place last night!'

'Really.' Blain was suddenly embarrassed by his brother's speculations. 'You're teasing me, Moylan. They probably felt sorry for me. What about this gunfight? Are you determined to go through with it?'

'Look Blain, that fellow Lecroy is a coward and a spoilt brat. It ain't me that won't go through with it. I ruined his fun and took his gun away. He'll not want a repeat performance. So stop worrying about me, and worry about where our next job is coming from.'

3

Blain lounged against the bar, one hand in his pocket, the other holding a beer. He wondered where Moylan was, and asked the barman if he had seen him.

'He left a while back. That big black fellow, Tomas, as works at the bordello came for him.'

'Did he say where they were going?'

'No. He and Tomas talked for a time, and then they left.'

Blain was frowning, trying to make sense of it all. And then it hit him: Moylan had deliberately dodged him. He had gone with Tomas to the gunfight, leaving him behind.

Blain's frantic hammering on the door of the brothel brought a tousle-haired young woman to the door.

'Tomas? He ain't here, or Miss Agatha,' she said, in answer to his urgent queries. 'Do you want to come in?'

She held the door open and he stepped inside.

'I need to find out where Tomas and my brother went. Did you see him this morning? Was he with Moylan?'

'No, I ain't see them. Adele's inside, maybe she knows.'

Adele, a coffee-coloured young beauty, had an anxious look when he queried about Tomas and Moylan's whereabouts. It turned out she was cousin to Tomas, and he had confided in her before leaving. She confirmed Blain's worst suspicions. He had left the house to collect Moylan and accompany him to the gunfight.

'There's an abandoned homestead a few mile out of town. That's where they're to meet.'

'What about Agatha, was she with them?'

'Agatha took Dessie to the sawbones. She was worried about her back going bad.'

What was he to do? He had to stop Moylan from participating in the gunfight, no matter what. The site of the duel was a few miles outside town. He had to get out there as soon as possible.

Blain was almost running as he headed to the livery where his horse was stabled. Twenty minutes of hard riding and he was approaching the homestead. There was no sign of activity and he thought he was too late. In a moment of despair he shouted out.

'Hang on Moylan, I'm coming!'

Then he saw the horses tethered in the yard. Blain pulled up and jumped from his mount, tied it alongside the others. Running into the yard he saw a group of people out on the pasture. As he hurried across he could see Lecroy and Moylan standing face to face. There were other men standing around the pair.

'Moylan,' he yelled.

'Blain!' Moylan exclaimed. 'You shouldn't have come here.'

As Blain went to join Moylan, the two men from last night

stepped forward and grabbed him.

'That's far enough, fella.'

'Blain, go back to town,' Moylan called. 'This ain't no place for you.'

'I'll go back if you come with me. I ain't going without you.'

'I should have known better than to come up here with a damned saddle bum,' Lecroy sneered. 'Do you want to cry off and run back home with your girlfriend?'

'Please, Moylan,' Blain pleaded.

There were tears in his eyes and fear in his heart as he stared at his brother.

'You know I can't, Blain. I gotta see this through.'

'Keep that snivelling brat quiet,' Lecroy instructed his men. 'Now if you ain't already wet your britches, can we get on with this? The sooner I let some daylight into that carcase of yours, the sooner we can all go back to town and celebrate my shooting a stinking saddle bum.'

Moylan turned from Blain and put his attention on the man mocking him.

'You're all wind and piss, rich boy. Let's get to it.'

There was a cold sneer on Lecroy's face as he eyed his opponent. Blain saw Tomas standing some few feet away. There was a resigned look on the big man's countenance as he stared at the men at the centre of the conflict. Blain groaned. The men holding him tightened their grip on his arms.

'Not a peep from you,' the man on the left hissed in Blain's ear. 'I'll break your arm if you try to interfere.'

The antagonists squared off. Blain stared at the scene before him. He was helpless in the grip of his captors. He sagged forlornly as they held him fast. Tears streamed down his cheeks. He had a terrible feeling of impending doom as he watched.

4

Moylan wore a sardonic smile as he looked across the short distance to his challenger.

'I've already beaten you at fisticuffs, rich boy,' he said. 'Are you sure you want to go ahead with this?'

The sneer never left Lecroy's face.

'You are nothing but trash. I'll put you down like I would a rabid dog.'

'We'll see,' Moylan said.

Tomas stepped up.

'At the count of ten, you draw. Is that understood?'

Both men nodded. Moylan had a slight smile on his face while Lecroy wore his habitual sneer. Tomas stepped back out of the line of fire.

'Remember, on the count of ten. Only when I call ten can you reach for a weapon. Ready on my command! One!'

Blain was motionless, held firmly in the grip of Lecroy's henchmen. His tears had dried up, but the feeling of impending disaster hung heavy in his guts.

'Moylan,' he whispered. 'Dear God, don't let him hurt you.'

Time seemed suspended, the counting dragging on interminably.

'Six . . . seven . . eight . . .'

Roughly twenty paces apart. Draw your gun, line up the target, squeeze the trigger and hope to wound or kill your opponent.

'Nine.'

As the nine was called out, Lecroy drew. That scornful sneer was replaced by a malignant glint. His gun was out and firing as the umpire called out the final number.

'Ten.'

'Moylan!' Blain yelled, his shout coinciding with the report from Lecroy's weapon.

Moylan's head jerked forward as the lead ball punched him in the chest. His hand was gripping the butt of his gun, partway out of his holster. He sank to his knees as his legs gave way. Blain was staring at his stricken brother.

'No!'

The men each side of Blain had slackened their grip. With sudden and vicious strength Blain drove his heel into the shin of the man on the right, who yelled and danced away. The youngster swung his fist into the face of the second man. The stricken man jerked back and let go, the better to defend himself. Blain didn't wait, but ran forward.

'Moylan!'

He flung himself on his knees in the dirt beside his wounded brother. Moylan lay ominously still, his hand on the gun he never got to fire. Blood was seeping into his shirt. Blain was weeping as he reached out a trembling hand. Tentatively he touched the dark bristly hair on his brother's head.

'Moylan . . .' he whimpered.

A dark shadow appeared on the ground beside him. Blain looked up with sudden anger. The big, dark form of Tomas was staring down at him.

'Master Moylan, is he. . . ?'

Blain stared back at the big man, unable to say anything. His throat had closed up. He shook his head mutely. More footsteps. Blain looked up, and Tomas stepped back. Slowly Blain swivelled his head. The face of the man who had just killed his brother hovered above him.

'Sorry kid, it's the luck of the game. If he was foolish enough to fight, then he must expect to be hurt.'

'You drew before the end of the count. He didn't stand a chance. You pulled on nine. You murdered him.'

Lecroy's men were gathering around. They stared solemnly at Blain kneeling in the dirt.

'Nonsense. I was just faster. I warned him I was an expert pistol shot. But he wouldn't back down.'

'You lie!' Blain's voice was rising. 'You drew before the end of the count and shot him down in cold blood. I saw it. So did all these men.'

Blain gestured around him at the onlookers. Lecroy was frowning.

'That's just not true. You're unhinged by grief. You're imagining things.' He spread his hands out in an all-embracing gesture. 'Ask anyone here. The fight was fair and square.'

Blain stared back at him. Murmurs of agreement buzzed around him like a chorus.

'Fair and square,' was repeated.

Blain shook his head.

'It was murder,' he whispered.

His eyes tracked from the crimson stain on the dead man's shirt to the pistol partway out of the holster. Blain moved. The pistol felt cold in his hand. He raised it, staring at Lecroy, pointing the weapon. The crowd of men gaping at him – shrinking back – fear in Lecroy's eyes.

'What are you doing?'

'I'm avenging the death of my brother.'

Lecroy yelled in terror and turned to run. Blain pulled the trigger just as something crashed into him and knocked him face down in the dirt.

5

A heavy weight crushed Blain into the dirt. Someone was yelling.

'He shot me! He's killed me!'

Blain could scarcely breathe, the pressure on his back relentless. He could hear Lecroy's high-pitched, plaintive voice calling out.

'Oh my God, don't let me die out in this place. Help me, someone help me.'

Blain was twisting his head to see what was happening. He could hear the heavy breathing of the man who had jumped him as he shot Lecroy.

'Verne, it's all right. It's only a flesh wound,' someone said.

'Damn you, get off me,' Blain grunted, gasping for breath.

His struggle was attracting the attention of the men clustered round the whimpering Lecroy.

'Keep him there, Tomas.'

'Are you sure I'm going to be all right?' Lecroy pleaded.

'Yeah, yeah, it's only a flesh wound. We'll get you to the sawbones. He'll patch you up. You've nothing to worry about.'

'Oh thank God! Thank God!'

Boots walking across and stopping by Blain.

'Get something to tie his hands. Keep him safe.'

The pressure eased on his back. Hands roughly grabbing him. Rawhide lashing his wrists together. Brutal hands gripping him and pulling him upright. The men who had held him during the duel standing before him. One man holding him and his companion hitting Blain, a hard punch in the mouth.

He felt his lip split and his head bounced back. Blain gasped and another fist hit him in the stomach. As he bent over a knee came out of nowhere and crashed into his face, crushing his nose. He felt the pain course through his head. Warm blood flowed from his busted nose. He blinked and tears of pain mingled with the blood.

'You bastard! We'll kill you for that!'

Blain stared dazedly at his tormentors. They turned and looked over their shoulders. Auther was supporting Lecroy as he made his way haltingly towards them. There was blood on Lecroy's shirt. He held his hand against his side, his fingers covered in blood. At last he stood before Blain, face pale and drawn.

'You vile piece of horse dung, you'll pay for this.' Lecroy thrust his face closer. 'It was only by the grace of God you didn't kill me.'

'It was Tomas as saved you, Verne. He jumped on the kid.'

Lecroy's gaze slid past Blain.

'This true, Tomas?'

'Sure thing, Master Verne, I wouldn't let no harm come to you.'

Lecroy turned his attention back to Blain.

'Who are you anyway? What is that piece of trash to you?'

'You murdered him! You're a coward and a murderer!'

A backhanded slap snapped Blain's head to one side.

'Shut your lying mouth. We all saw what happened. The fight was fair and square. Your pal was too slow and paid for it with his life. He shouldn't have challenged Mr Lecroy. Now he's dead.'

Blain stared from face to face. The men gathered round him glared back with hard inflexible eyes.

'You are all guilty. You all helped murder him. How are you going to silence me? Are you going to murder me, too? I tell you now that's the only way you're going to stop me from telling the truth of what happened here today.'

Lecroy laughed, then winced abruptly as the wound in his side hurt. When he recovered he glared at Blain.

'I am a fair man,' Lecroy began, then stopped. He looked past Blain to Tomas. 'What's this whelp's name?'

'Blain Larkin, Mr Lecroy, he a brother to that there Moylan.'

'Listen, Blain Larkin, and listen well. You can yelp all you want. No one is going to believe you. All these men here are witness. It was a fair fight. Your brother died because he was too slow. As I say, I am a reasonable man. I will give you a choice. You can keep your damned mouth shut with those lies, and agree with these gentlemen that the fight was fair and square. If you consent to that, then I will forget you tried to murder me. I will tell everyone your brother put the bullet in me during the fight. That way your brother will have died with honour secure. He will get a decent burial and a fine headstone. What you say, eh?'

To Blain's amazement Lecroy proffered his hand.

'Let's shake on it, as gentlemen. We can both leave this place of blood with honour intact.'

Blain was staring at his tormentor, hardly believing what he was hearing.

'You murdered him, and you think I'll keep quiet about it? You murdered him! I saw you draw before the end of the count.'

'You young fool! Look around you. All these men saw what happened. They'll all swear the same. No one is going to believe a young puppy like you. This is your last chance. Will you take it?'

'Never!' Blain knew with certainty he could not let Moylan down. Blain could not live with that. 'Never,' he repeated. 'I'll swear in court what you did. They'll hang you for murder.'

Blain stared defiantly at the man who had shot Moylan.

22

Lecroy, with pale, drawn features and blood-soaked shirt, gazed moodily at the youth. He saw something in the boy's eyes that disconcerted him. It was the lack of fear in Blain's expression that captured his attention. For what seemed long, interminable minutes they stared at each other. Blain did not blink under that scrutiny. It was Lecroy who looked away first.

'Let's go,' he said, and turned away.

Leaning heavily on his companions, Lecroy slowly trekked across to the horses. Blain was roughly made to walk. His arms were bound, and the men on each side gripped him tightly as if to prevent him making a run for it. Blain had no thought of running. Numbed by the death of his beloved brother, he stumbled across the paddock, a hard ball of grief in the pit of his stomach.

6

'Let the prisoner stand to hear the sentence of the court.'

A rough hand jerked Blain to his feet. During the trial the evidence had piled up relentlessly against him. Every time he had tried to protest his innocence he had been ruthlessly silenced. He had shouted and ranted at the court officials as the distortions of the case escalated. At one stage the judge had ordered the deputies to take Blain back to the cells until he calmed down. Worn down by the sheer weight of slander and misrepresentation of the facts, Blain had been reduced to numbed submission. One by one, Verne Lecroy's friends had come forward and perjured themselves.

'The facts speak for themselves,' the judge continued. 'On

14 April 1878 you accompanied one Moylan Larkin for the purpose of inciting him into fighting a duel. In spite of imprecations and pleas for reconciliation from the offended party you urged the unfortunate Moylan Larkin to fight. In the course of the confrontation your brother was shot and mortally wounded. You did then maliciously take it upon yourself to exact revenge for this act, and pulled a pistol and shot and wounded the said Verne Lecroy. It has also been stated by witnesses that you swore your intention was to kill Lecroy. It saddens me that one so young has ended up in this predicament. . . .'

Blain stared impassively out the window of the courtroom. He hardly heard the words of the judge. After the days of lies and perjury from a succession of witnesses his resistance was broken. Now he endured in stupefied silence.

In dazed perplexity, the events of the court washed over Blain. He dared not look to where Todd Potts, his defence lawyer, sat. The lawyer had visited Blain in the cells, and after listening to his protestations of innocence, had told him it would be better to plead guilty. Gradually Blain's attention shifted, and he tried to pay attention to the man who had the power of life and death over him.

'Therefore in view of the evidence in front of me it is my sad duty to pass the ultimate sentence upon you.'

Blain watched with detached interest as the judge picked up some dark object from the bench. With solemn pomposity he placed the black fabric on his head.

'Blain Larkin, it is the verdict of this court that on the sixteenth of May you will be taken to a place of execution and hanged by the neck until dead. May God have mercy on your soul.'

'All stand for the judge.'

There was a rustle of movement and a babble of voices broke out. Blain did not have time to see more. He was dragged from the dock and returned to the cell that had been his home during the weeks of his incarceration. Blain flung himself on the bunk and wept.

Now that his fate had been decided, Blain retreated into a world of mute fear. His frantic mind played constantly over the happenings of the past weeks. Events jumbled together until he hardly knew what was real and what were the products of his fevered imagination. What little sleep he managed was filled with nightmare images of bloody carcases. Blain would wake sweating with dread.

'I'm only sixteen, I don't wanna die.'

The tears would come and he would sob out his fears far into the lonely, anxiety-ridden nights.

The clanging of keys and metal doors clashing interrupted his maudlin thoughts. He listened to the footsteps of the deputy as he approached. A sturdy wood truncheon banged against the bars of his cell. He had been expecting the assault on the bars but it still made him jump.

'Larkin, visitor!'

The deputy, a stout individual with mutton-chop whiskers, gave one final rattle on the bars, then stepped back to allow the visitor to approach. It was Todd Potts, his lawyer. Blain stood and greeted him.

'Is there any news?'

'There is to be a stay of execution.'

'A stay of execution! Does that mean they're not going to hang me?'

'There is no hangman in the town of Callender.'

'I am not to die, not yet. Perhaps you will get a pardon for me.'

Potts looked down at his boots.

'I am doing all I can. You are to be transferred to Ablecreek. They have a hangman there.'

Blain turned his back on the two men so they could not see

the despair in his eyes. He sank on his bunk, fresh waves of misery threatening to unman him in front of the jailor and the lawyer.

It wasn't until two days later that Blain had another visitor.

'Your sister is here to see you, Larkin.'

The deputy was grinning agreeably, which was unusual. For the most part his jailors were surly brutes showing no sympathy or gentleness towards their charge. Blain was bewildered. He had no sisters. The guard motioned a young woman forward. Blain blinked in surprise.

'Blain, my dearest brother, I persuaded Mother to let me come. Sorry I didn't arrive earlier, but I've been unwell. My injured back, you know.'

She smiled sweetly at him. Blain stared at the young woman, his mouth agape. She was elegantly dressed in a dark blue crinoline dress. A saucy hat of matching colour perched atop her head.

'I hope your turn in prison ain't made you forget your dear sister, Dessie.'

'Dessie,' Blain breathed the name. 'No, of course not. I . . . I've not forgotten you.'

The last time Blain saw Dessie she was laying on a bed weeping, while he washed blood from her back where Verne Lecroy had slashed her with his riding whip.

'It's so terrible. I can hardly believe what is happening to you,' Dessie said.

She moved forwards as if to reach out to Blain.

'No contact, Miss, if you please.'

Dessie turned to face the guard. She placed her hands behind her back. As Blain watched, the butt of a small pistol slid from the sleeve of her dress.

'What, am I not allowed one little caress from my dear brother?'

As Dessie spoke she was smiling coquettishly at the guard.

26

At the same time she was inching closer and closer to the bars of the cell. The guard, a middle-aged man with heavy jowls and a luxuriant moustache, had all his attention on her. Females were a rarity at the prison. Ones as young and tasty as this were unknown.

Blain stared hypnotized at the pearl butt of the small weapon. He was afraid to move. He shot a glance at the guard. The man's eyes were fixed on Dessie. Blain slid to his knees on to the stone floor. The fullness of Dessie's dress hid him from the guard. He reached forward.

'Are you a married man, Captain?'

The guard made a sour face.

'Er . . . no . . . I ain't married.'

She felt the tug on her sleeve as the pistol was taken.

'I can hardly believe that some woman hasn't snapped you up long ago.'

Blain stuffed the pocket gun inside his shirt. Slowly he stood.

'Sister, is there any message from Mother?' he asked.

Dessie turned back to the prisoner.

'Mother tells me nothing. All she does is weep for her poor boy. She wanted to come herself, but couldn't face to see you in such a place. We're all so sorry about what happened. Poor Moylan, he was so brave. We'll never forget what he did for us.'

When she departed, Blain took out the small gun and examined it. The weapon was an up-and-over Derringer. Holding it in his hand he lay there thinking about it. Dessie had risked a lot to get the weapon to him. If she had been caught it would have meant a spell in prison at least.

He had no idea what he was supposed to use the Derringer for. Certainly he could not imagine breaking out of his prison cell with just a pocket gun as a weapon.

The next day they came for him and put manacles on his

wrists and ankles and escorted him from the jail. He was being transferred to Ablecreek where the hangman awaited.

7

'Larkin.'

Blain heard his name whispered and opened his eyes, not knowing where he was. Then he felt the rocking of the railroad wagon and reality came crashing back.

'Larkin, are you awake? Our guard has dozed off.'

Blain lay on the hard floor of the wagon blinking the sleep from his eyes.

'Yeah, I'm awake. What's your name?'

'Jephta Owens. You and me, Larkin, we're for the high jump.'

There were just the two prisoners. For security they wore manacles on wrists and ankles. An armed marshal had been appointed as their escort. The marshal was heavily built with dark curly hair. At the beginning of the journey he had explained the rules.

'I'm Marshal Bill Neagle. I'm to deliver you rats to Ablecreek. No talking. No spitting.' He then patted the large pistol he carried. 'If you try anything I shoot you.'

Blain examined his fellow prisoner. The only light came from a barred skylight in the roof of the van and another in the door that communicated with the next wagon. As far as he could tell his fellow prisoner was not much older than he was. The youngster had a habit of keeping his chin tucked in and staring at everything from beneath lowered eyebrows. It gave him the wily look of a fox or coyote waiting the chance to pounce on whatever stray victim came his way. Blain thought about the remark his companion had made.

'The high jump?' he whispered back. 'What do you mean?'

'They've sent for Bullock,' the youngster answered. 'You know about Bullock?'

'No.'

'The best hangman in the west. That's why they're sending us to Ablecreek, so as Bullock can hang us.'

Blain did not like the way the conversation was going. He tried to divert his companion by asking about how he came to be tangled up with the law.

'Jephta, what did you do?'

'I killed a fella. Ripped his rotten guts out. Is it true you tried to murder Verne Lecroy?'

'Yeah, it's true.'

'Sure wish I'd 'a been there to see that. You hurt him bad?'

'Some. He had a hole in his side. He was fit enough to come into court and tell a passel of lies about me.'

'Nobody tells the truth in court. They all lie. The judge lies. The lawyers lie. The witnesses lie. Don't pay to tell the truth, no how. I was supposed to go last week, but then they got hold of you and decided to dangle us together.'

In spite of his own distress, Blain was intrigued. Owens seemed quite sanguine about his fate.

'The thought of being hanged doesn't seem to bother you much,' he whispered back.

'The way I figure, I ain't hanged yet. It's a long way to Ablecreek. If a chance comes along to make a run for it I mean to take it.'

'What about the guard? What if he starts shooting?'

'What's the difference?' Owens whispered. 'They gonna hang me anyway. I'd as soon take my chances dodging a bullet as a rope. Are you with me, Larkin? Two stand a better chance than one on his own.'

Jephta Owens's fatalistic approach affected Blain.

I am an outcast because I crossed a man who has influence and wealth, he thought. I did nothing wrong, and yet I am to be executed. He knew Jephta was right. He would take a leaf out of his companion's book. Not for him anymore the submissive acceptance of his fate. If he were to die then he would go down fighting.

'Larkin! What do you say?'

His companion hissed out the words, thinking Blain was not going to answer.

'Yeah, I'm with you.'

There was a sudden movement from the marshal. He jerked upright as he came awake.

'What's going on? Are you fellas talking?'

With a grunt he came off the sack of mail he had been using as a resting place. He grabbed up his pistol and swung it. There was an audible clump as the barrel hit Jephta on the side of the head. The youngster yelped and fell sideways. It was obvious to Blain he was to be the next target. He watched the swing of the gun and rolled back as it hit him. The blow glanced off the side of his head, rather than make solid contact. It stung but did not stun. But Neagle was not to be fooled.

'Damn you, you piece of dung!'

This time Blain could not avoid the pistol. It cracked against his head just above his ear. The force of the blow drove his head against the side of the carriage. The top of Blain's head exploded with even greater pain as the pistol bounced off his skull. He tried to put his hands up to protect himself, but the guard brushed his manacled hands aside with a brutal swipe of his improvised club. Blain cried out as his knuckles took the full force of the blow. He cowered down as the marshal relentlessly battered him, hitting out indiscriminately at head and body.

Blain squirmed around and rolled on the floor, trying to avoid the worst of the brutal beating. Satisfied he had restored discipline, the burly guard turned and settled back on his seat.

'Next time I'll use the butt end to break your skulls open,' he growled.

Blain could feel blood oozing from cuts on his head. He lay slumped on the floor holding his hands to his injuries, moaning softly. As he lay there suffering, Blain felt the Derringer hidden inside his shirt pressing against his skin.

I could take this out and shoot that brute, he thought. He had tried to kill a man once before. That had been in the hot rage of vengeance. He wondered when next the opportunity came if he would be able to use the little gun with any more success.

As Blain lay on the floor of the carriage, he listened to the clack of the wheels as the train rumbled on towards Ablecreek and the gallows. Jephta Owens had intimated he would make a run for it should the chance arise. If such an opportunity came his way then Blain was determined he would also go.

The pain in his body grew. His anger and resentment grew also. Each rattle of the train wheels, taking him nearer and nearer to Ablecreek and the hangman's noose, increased his resolution to make a break for it should the opportunity arise.

The Lecroy family home was a lavish mansion surrounded by landscaped gardens. Servants provided the needs of the family inside the house, while gardeners tended to the outside. The head of the family, Mortimer Lecroy, was working in his study when his son walked in.

'You wanted to see me, Father?'

Lecroy waved a hand at his son.

'Take a seat, Verne. I'll be finished this in a moment or two.'

The younger Lecroy wandered over to a glass drinks cabinet and opened it.

'You want a drink, Father?'

'I suppose a shot of bourbon wouldn't go amiss.'

Verne poured the drinks, helping himself to a large glass of brandy. When he set the bourbon on the desk his father looked up at the brimming brandy glass.

'You drink too much, Verne.'

'Only because I'm bored.'

With a sigh the older man set his papers aside and contemplated his only son. Mortimer Lecroy was a stern-looking man of middle age, with greying hair and matching well-trimmed beard and moustache. His face was narrow with a long hooked nose.

'Was it boredom that caused that trouble over Larkin?'

'No Father, you know what happened. Those saddle-bums set out to murder me. You're lucky to still have a son and heir to take over all your worldly goods.' Verne walked across to the window and with his back to his father emptied the brandy glass. 'I don't know why you're bothered about those troublemaking bastards.'

Mortimer Lecroy's face took on an angry tinge.

'You ungrateful pup! Time and again I've had to use my influence to get you out of trouble. It has cost me plenty to pay those witnesses to perjure themselves on your behalf.

'Anyway, we should be free of the Larkins now. The last one is on his way to be hanged and that should be the end of the matter.'

Verne returned to the drinks and poured another brandy. His Father watched with an exasperated look on his face.

'For God's sake Verne, go easy on the brandy.'

'Why Father, are supplies running low? Perhaps I should go out to a saloon for a drink.'

Mortimer Lecroy bit down his anger. Verne was his only son, and though he'd had no direct hand in his upbringing, he had allowed the boy to be spoiled by his mother and then by a succession of governesses.

'It's time you were married and settled down. The responsibility of a wife and family would be a steadying influence. Aren't there any young women that take your fancy?'

'Oh dear me, Father, I'm much too young for that. At twenty-five I've still a lot of wild oats to sow. Wait until I'm middle-aged.'

'You're damned well too eager to sow wild oats as you call it. You need something to occupy you. That's what I called you in here today to talk about.'

Verne feigned to look at his father with mock horror.

'I'm sincerely hoping you're not proposing for me to take up employment of some kind. I'd not cut out for that sort of thing.'

He helped himself to a cigar from the box on the desk.

'No, I don't suppose you are,' his father sighed. 'What I'm

proposing is something completely different. This latest shooting escapade with those cowboys put it in my mind.'

The smoke from his son's cigar drifted across the desk. Mortimer paused from speaking while he reached over and lit one for himself. Father and son sat across from each other, cigar smoke drifting lazily into the room.

'I'm proposing you go out west and supervise our bank in Crow's Butte.'

'Me! What the hell do I know about banking?'

'You'll have experienced clerks to take care of all the details for you. You will be there only as my representative.'

'An important businessman in Crow's Butte. I could end up like you and have my own business empire.'

'That's what I'm hoping, son.'

Before father and son could fantasize any more there was a discreet knock on the study door. The door opened and a head peered round.

'Mr Tex Plant to see you, sir.'

'Plant! Yes, yes! Show him in.'

The door opened fully and a man dressed in black stepped inside. He was still a young man, not yet forty. His broad handsome face was spoiled somewhat by his eyes, cold and calculating as he surveyed the two men in the room. Mortimer was on his feet coming round the desk, hand outstretched.

'Mr Plant, it is a real pleasure to welcome you to my home. This is my son, Verne. You and he will work together.'

The men eyed each other as they shook hands, one the spoiled child of a rich influential father, the other the product of a military background. Tex Plant had been a captain in the cavalry before he was kicked out for killing a fellow officer in an argument. Now he was a gun for hire. And Mortimer Lecroy had hired him as bodyguard and companion for his son.

9

Marshal Neagle was hammering on the door of the van to attract the attention of the railroad conductor riding in the next carriage. The door slid back and a man in a railroad uniform with a peaked cap appeared in the opening.

'Yeah,' he asked, 'what's all the fuss about?'

'Where the hell are we? I'm locked in here with these two hellions. I might as well be in a cattle truck for all I can see.'

'We're just outside Cripple Peak. We'll be stopping to take on water.'

'Damn it all, Hayden, I reckon when we stop I ought to go outside and stretch my legs.'

'What about those two? They giving any bother?'

'Nah, everything's under control.'

'Tell you what, Bill, why don't you come in here with me? I got a bottle.'

'That'll sure be one welcome drink.'

The train was slowing more and more as they approached the outskirts of Cripple Peak. Before stepping through to join the railroad guard, Neagle turned and glared at the two youngsters. He pulled his pistol and brandished it in their direction.

'One word, just one word from you, and I'll be back in here and beat you senseless. Understand? When we get to Ablecreek there won't be no need for no hanging, they'll just need to bury you.'

There was a loud screeching as brakes locked on the wheels. The heavy locomotive jerked and slowed, tossing the man in the doorway against the frame.

'Damn it!' he swore, and disappeared.

The heavy door slammed to with a crash, leaving the prisoners alone.

'I'd like to be free of these chains with a good knife,' Jephta hissed. 'I'd cut that booger's heart out and feed it to him.'

'How's your head?' Blain asked, keeping his voice low.

'Probably cracked my skull the way he hit me. You OK?'

'I think I'd rather be hanged as take another beating like that.'

The train was almost at a standstill. The carriage jerked and couplings clanked, and a loud hissing could be heard as steam was vented under pressure. Then there came another sound over and above the noise of the train. The prisoners strained to make out what was going on. They heard popping sounds and faint shouts in the distance.

'Gunshots!' Blain exclaimed, 'Maybe someone is holding up the train.'

They craned towards the side of the carriage, listening to the noise and trying to make out what was happening.

'They're attacking the train,' a voice yelled.

The prisoners clambered to their feet and pressed their ears against the thick wood panels of their carriage.

'This could be our chance,' Jephta exclaimed. 'If we could jump the marshal and make a break for it. With all that's going on we'll get away in the confusion.'

'What about these chains?'

Blain held up his hands, the chain dangling from the wristbands.

'Hell, we'll worry about that when we get away. We just gotta take whatever chance comes our way.'

'Jephta, we got an ace in the hole,' Blain told him. 'I got me a gun!'

'A gun, what the hell you saying?'

By way of answer, Blain put his hand inside his shirt and withdrew the small weapon. Jephta stared at the Derringer. Excitement showed in his face.

'You goddamn freak, Larkin. How the hell you do that?'

His glance slid to the door as if he had heard something. The voices outside were discussing the shooting, the men wondering if they should go up the tracks to assist.

'Quick Blain, here's what we do. We pretend to fight. Shout and yell and jump about. When that marshal comes back in he'll start swinging that pistol at us. When he's close enough I'll jump him and you shove that gun in his face.'

As he finished speaking Jephta kicked his heel against the side of the wagon.

'Start yelling!' he called.

Blain was scared, but he drew in a deep breath and bellowed as loud as his hurting head would allow. They didn't have long to wait: the heavy door of the carriage banged open, and Neagle stood framed in the doorway. He had his pistol out and was pointing it at Blain.

'What the hell's going on?' he snarled. 'I ought'a shoot you now and save myself any more bother. Hell if I won't.'

10

Blain gaped at the marshal, his hand by his side gripping the Derringer. He stared in sheer terror at the big pistol in the deputy's hand.

Just out of sight of the lawman, Jephta was pressed against

the wall of the carriage, his eye on that hand extended inside the baggage car holding the pistol. He had expected the marshal to rush in and start beating Blain. That would have been his chance to jump the marshal while Blain shoved the gun on him. All he could see was the hand holding the pistol. And Neagle didn't appear to be coming any further.

'Goddamn you, Larkin, you've caused me enough trouble.'

Then Jephta smelt it, the strong smell of alcohol. Evidently Neagle and the railroad guard had been sharing a bottle.

Outside the shouts and the firing was still going on. Jephta stared at the hand with the pistol, willing the deputy to come further inside. To his consternation he saw the hammer thumbed back.

'You just can't wait for the hangman, can you, Larkin. Now it looks as if I have to finish off what Lecroy started back in Callender.'

Blain was staring at the gun as if hypnotised. In his fright he had all but forgotten the small gun clutched in his sweaty hand.

'Die, you lousy lizard!'

In desperation Jephta sprang into action. A short chain about fifteen inches long connected the manacles on his wrists. The youngster looped the chain around the gun. With a quick jerk he pulled down. Two things happened. The gun went off with an ear-cracking detonation as the marshal was dragged inside the baggage car. Fortunately it was aimed at the floor and the bullet buried itself in the floorboards. Jephta heaved on the marshal's arm, throwing him off balance.

'Damn your rotten hide!' Neagle yelled, as he was pulled inside.

With his free arm the marshal swung a roundhouse at Jephta, catching him on the ear. Valiantly the youngster ignored the punch and hung on to the chain, effectively trapping Neagle's gun arm.

'Blain!' Jephta yelled, 'shoot the booger!'

The cry shook Blain out of his funk. He rushed forwards, bringing up his weapon. Neagle saw him coming, and with a tremendous effort swung around, dragging Jephta with him. As Blain was bringing up the Derringer, the marshal struck out. His fist smashed Blain in the jaw and sent him reeling. The hand holding the Derringer jolted against the doorframe, and with a cry Blain lost his grip on the weapon. The little gun disappeared somewhere outside. Blain crumpled to the floor, his senses reeling.

Seeing Blain out of the fight, the marshal turned his attention to Jephta. With a snarl he raised his fist and drove it into Jephta's face. The youngster was desperately trying to free himself from Neagle, but the chain he had thought to use as a weapon now held him tethered to his attacker.

Again and again the marshal drove his clenched fist into Jephta's unprotected face. Blood was flowing freely from his nose and mouth. There was blood on his shirt as the marshal bludgeoned him. Seeing the youngster had no more fight in him, Neagle took the time to extricate his trapped arm.

His head buzzing with pain, Blain crawled towards the combatants, his bruised hand a throbbing ache. Just as Blain reached him the marshal's hand came free. Jephta was lying helpless on the floor, his face a bloody mess. Catching sight of Blain almost upon him, Neagle turned around and brought up the gun once more.

'Goddamn rats,' he yelled. 'You're both dead!'

In desperation Blain grabbed for the marshal's boot and yanked. Seeing Blain back in the fight gave Jephta a second wind. He kicked out wildly. His stout prison shoe hit the marshal's arm and jerked it upwards as he pulled the trigger. At that moment the conductor came through with a shotgun levelled at the tangle of bodies.

Neagle's gun went off, the bullet hitting the newcomer in the chest. The conductor bellowed and involuntarily pulled the trigger of his shotgun as he fell back. There was a tremendous blast of flame and smoke from the muzzle. Most of the lead shot took Neagle in the neck and head. He crashed back, blood erupting from his ruined face.

The explosions were deafening inside the confines of the carriage, shocking the combatants into stillness. By the door, the railroad man lay on the floor moaning, holding his hands across the wound in his chest, blood seeping through his fingers. Neagle was very dead, lying in a pool of blood, his face a red pulp.

Jephta climbed dazedly to his feet. The youngsters stared at each other, not quite sure what to do next. It was Jephta who regained some sense of purpose.

'Grab that shotgun,' he shouted, and bent to pick up Neagle's weapon.

'Help me,' the conductor moaned.

Blain stared at the wounded man, unable to move. Jephta pushed him.

'The shotgun,' he hissed again.

Jerked out of his torpor Blain grabbed the shotgun.

'What about the conductor? We have to help him.'

Jephta was pushing Blain towards the doorway. He tried to protest, but Jephta relentlessly bullied him through the door. The next carriage was empty, with the door to the outside lying open.

Cautiously they peered outside. The platform in their immediate vicinity was empty. The shooting they had heard earlier had ceased.

'Let's go.'

Jephta jumped to the platform and headed across to the opposite side. They jumped on to the tracks. A few deserted carriages stood on the rails. The pair shuffled along past the stationary carriages and towards the outbuildings that held workshops and storehouses, the chains on their ankles hindering fast walking. They shambled along, eyes alert for danger – two desperate youngsters splattered in blood, one carrying a shotgun and the other brandishing a pistol.

11

The fugitives made their way past deserted sheds, having to thread their way through an assortment of machinery stacked alongside iron rails and barrels and coils of wire. Hearing voices ahead the fugitives crept forwards and spied two men crouched behind a large water tank. They were holding revolvers and peering underneath the tank at something on the other side.

'How many more barrels?' a voice called from up ahead.

'There's at least half a dozen more.'

At that point the two men in hiding stepped into the open.

'Hold it! Hands in the air. We're the law.'

To emphasize the order the speaker fired a shot in the air. Blain and Jephta crept closer. Beyond the tank they could see a wagon. Two men were in the act of loading a cask into it. A third man stood by the rear wheel. As he was the only man with his hands free he raised them slowly above his head. The men caught with the barrel were in a quandary. It was obvious they were reluctant to let go their burden, and hesitated uncertainly. The lawmen walked forwards. Both were dressed in wool suits with Derbys on their heads.

41

'What the hell is this?' the man standing by the wheel blustered. He was a youngish man, hatless, with dark hair swept back from his forehead. 'We're law-abiding citizens! No need for guns.'

'Oh, we know what you are, all right. We've been watching you for a while. Your little game's been rumbled. Stealing bourbon. You're all under arrest. Clever ploy to distract us by having someone shoot up the front of the train.'

'Dammit, this is kerosene. We've got the papers. Come and have a look.'

The man by the wagon wheel half turned to his companions stuck at the back of the wagon with the barrel.

'Set that down and show him.'

'One wrong move and we start shooting. Drop any weapons you have. Don't matter to us if we take you in dead or alive.'

'Let's help these fellas,' Jephta hissed. 'Seeing as they're on the wrong side of the law they'll more an' likely help us in return.'

'How?'

For answer Jephta pointed to the shotgun in Blain was carrying.

'You take the one on the right. I'll handle the one on the left.'

Jephta hefted the pistol and stepped out from behind the tank. Blain followed, his shotgun levelled.

'OK, you fellas, we got you covered,' Jephta yelled. 'Drop those guns.'

Everything happened at once. The men holding the barrel let it fall. The man on the far side must have been holding his pistol ready and he fired off a shot at the lawmen. At the same time one of the detectives whirled around and fired at Jephta and Blain. The other was mouthing curses and shooting at the men by the wagon.

The gunman by the wagon yelled out and tumbled backwards as the bullets from the detective hit him. His companion took cover and fired back. The spokesperson for the trio rolled beneath the wagon, pulled a pistol and joined in the shooting.

Blain was pointing the shotgun at the lawmen with his finger on the trigger. He froze up as one swivelled around and emptied his pistol at them.

Jephta cried out and fell back. Blain was turning towards him when a bullet hit his manacles, almost knocking the shotgun from his grasp. His hands tightened on the weapon as he felt the shock, and inadvertently he pulled the trigger. The gun went off, and the recoil knocked Blain from his feet. The youngster pushed himself upright. Jephta was sitting against one of the wooden stanchions holding his arm. A dark stain was spreading on his sleeve.

'Jephta, you're hurt.'

Blain crawled to his companion.

'Hurts like hell,' Jephta grunted. 'Bastard got me in the arm.'

By now the shooting had died down. Blain heard footsteps approaching and belatedly grabbed for the shotgun. One of the men from the wagon stopped before them. He held a pistol in one hand but spaced his arms wide in a gesture of peace.

'Whoa friend, I got nothing against you. In fact just the opposite. Those fellas had us cold when you showed up.'

It was the young man who had tried to sidetrack the lawmen. His quick, intelligent eyes took in the state of the youngsters, noting the manacled wrists and ankles.

'I'll be doggone, looks like you're on the run. Come on, you'd better stick with us. We'll get you to a safe place. We owe you that after what you did.'

He holstered his revolver, then bent over Blain.

'Where you hit fella?'

'I don't rightly know. Jephta here's been hit in the arm.'

'Let me help. The sooner we're away from here the better. That shooting might attract attention.'

The stranger bent over and assisted Blain to his feet.

'Where does it hurt, fella?'

'I . . . I don't feel nothing.'

Blain was examining himself wondering if the bullet had destroyed all feeling. The newcomer noted the twisted manacle. He put out his hand and pointed to the bullet lodged in the link.

'You're one lucky son of a bitch,' he exclaimed. 'That bullet could have finished you. Can you walk?'

'Yeah.'

'Go on over to the wagon. I'll look after your buddy.'

Blain started forwards, then came to an abrupt halt. One of the lawmen was lying in the dirt looking very dead. His companion lay beside him groaning. Where his legs had been was a bloody mess of raw flesh and white, exposed bone.

'Help me,' the man moaned. 'Oh God, help me.'

Blain could not move. He stood there gaping at the lawman's mangled legs. He had a horrible feeling his shotgun had done the damage.

'Damn it fella, keep moving,' a voice urged him from behind. 'The sooner we're away from here the better.'

'What about him?' Blain stammered.

'He's beyond help. Now move.'

Blain was pushed from behind.

'You wanna stay, then you stay. We're moving out.'

'Sons of bitches, you gotta help me!' the man suddenly found the strength to shriek at them.

By now Jephta had reached the wagon and leaned against it. The two surviving members of the team bent over the body of their companion lying in the dirt.

'Dammit, Kersterson's dead. Hell's curses on those Pinkertons.'

Blain was still traumatized by the knowledge that it was he who had shot and wounded the lawman.

'Jephta, we gotta help him,' he pleaded.

Nursing his wounded arm Jephta glared at Blain.

'Help him, sure I'll help.' Jephta still held the big pistol he had taken from the dead marshal. 'That's the sonabitch as shot me,' he yelled. 'You want me to help him? Sure I will.'

He pointed the gun at the moaning man.

'No!'

Blain's shout came too late. The gun in Jephta's hand belched flame. There was a sharp explosion and a hole appeared in the wounded man's head. The body twitched and the moaning stopped.

'Now can we get on?' Jephta yelled.

Blain was staring in horror at the dead bodies. Then someone was pulling him towards the wagon. He kept looking back at the dead lawmen sprawled in the dirt. They bundled him inside the wagon. He lay on top of the casks. There were tears in his eyes.

12

Verne Lecroy groaned and turned over. Resting on the pillow beside him a tangled mass of blonde hair.

'Oh, my goddamn aching head.' He reached up and massaged his forehead. 'Wake up, you cow,' he growled at the female lying beside him. 'What the hell happened last night? How the blazes did I get here?'

There was no response from his companion. Verne threw back the bed covers and drove his elbow into the woman's ribs. She didn't flinch. Suffering with throbbing head and nausea, Verne was becoming angry.

He swivelled around and putting his feet against the woman shoved. She tumbled from the bed on to the floor. Even in his inebriated state Lecroy wondered at the coldness of her body.

'It's like being in bed with a corpse,' he muttered.

He peered over at the young woman on the floor. She had landed on her back, her naked body sprawled carelessly. Her blonde tresses had fallen back from her face. For moments Verne stared in shock, a cold feeling creeping over him.

'What. . . !'

Her face was greyish and mottled. A blackened tongue protruded from her mouth. Around her neck was a cord tied so tightly it was almost buried in the flesh. Abruptly Verne hauled himself back into the bed. He lay on his back, trembling.

'What happened?' he whispered.

He could remember very little of the previous night. There was the dinner at the family home attended by the pompous dignitaries invited by his father. Verne had felt ill at ease amongst the elderly men who had attended. He'd had to listen to tedious tales of valour related by middle-aged men as they relived their youthful past.

In order to alleviate the boredom and disguise his loathing, Verne had drunk more and more wine and then moved on to the brandy. After that things became hazy. Now he had awakened to find himself sharing a bed with a dead whore.

Verne clambered from the bed. With trembling hands he got dressed. He failed to notice his necktie was missing. If he had been more alert he might have realized the missing item was tied around the throat of the young woman lying out of his sight on the other side of the bed.

Once dressed, Verne crossed the room, averting his eyes from the gruesome figure sprawled on the floor. Cautiously he opened the door. The corridor was empty.

He was remembering where he was now. This was the very same brothel where Moylan Larkin, the obnoxious cowboy, had attacked him. Verne closed the door behind him. He tried to tread gently on the stairs. However, his efforts at stealth were futile, and Agatha, the madam of the house, stepped from the parlour as he descended.

'Good morning, Master Lecroy.' She was about to ask how he was, but decided against it when she noted the pasty face and hollow eyes with dark pouches beneath. 'Everything to your satisfaction?'

He stared at her, his mouth working, not making any sound. With something between a snarl and a grunt he brushed past her and made for the front door. Agatha watched him go, a look of extreme distaste on her face.

'It takes wealth and breeding to make a man into a boor and a bully,' she muttered.

Verne stumbled along the street, oblivious to his surroundings. The image of the dead girl was imposed on his mind, and he could not shake off his feelings of dread. Eventually he stopped and leaned against a gable wall, trying to regain some control over his fear. All sorts of jumbled thoughts crowded in, now that he had paused in his retreat from the brothel.

What would happen when the body of the girl was found? He would be accused of her murder. How would he evade the consequences of his actions? He could flee, but where would he go? He would have to return home to collect belongings, and then he would need money.

Verne had never worried about money. He ran up bills in

brothels and gambling dens, and was seldom troubled about paying his way. Often times he reneged on his debts. In most cases the people he owed were afraid to accuse the son of Mortimer Lecroy.

If he ran from Callender his source of wealth would be cut off. Verne had been in numerous scrapes over the years, and in the past Mortimer Lecroy had always come through for his son. Verne had killed men in gunfights and wounded others in separate incidents before the killing of Moylan Larkin. Each time he had escaped the consequences of his actions. Why should this time be any different?

As he worried over these issues Verne's natural cunning took over. A measure of calm returned. In the end, what it would boil down to was his word against the people in the brothel.

Back at the brothel, Agatha finished her morning repast. She summoned a young girl to clear away the breakfast things.

'And when you have finished in the kitchen go and tell Bella I want to see her. That is, if she's in a fit state to come down. She was in room seven with that depraved creature, Lecroy. I don't suppose he paid her, but one can always live in hope.'

With that she settled down to read a slim paperbound book. There was a lurid drawing on the front depicting a bear of a man fighting several half-naked savages. Agatha was not far into her book when she was interrupted by screams from the upper floor. Hurriedly she put her book down and made her way out of the parlour. As she hastened upstairs, the screaming continued. The girl was in the doorway of one of the rooms with her hands to her mouth, staring wide-eyed at something inside.

'Loula,' Agatha shouted, 'cut out that goddamned cater-wauling.'

Loula continued to scream until Agatha reached her and slapped her hard on the cheek. The screams changed to sobbing. Agatha stared at the dead girl lying inside the bedroom.

'Bella, oh my poor Bella!'

Agatha had to prop herself against the door, her face pale, her breathing short and agitated. Her hand was at her neck as she stared at her dead girl.

'Lecroy,' she said, her voice barely above a whisper. 'Oh, dear God, Lecroy.'

13

Normally Agatha allowed her girls to sleep in the morning, but with the tragic turn of events that was now impossible. They gathered around the doorway staring with varying expressions of distress. In the midst of the confusion Agatha embarked on a strategy to mitigate the harm she knew was coming at her with this tragic death. Tomas her houseman had been summoned.

'Tomas, come inside. I need you to help me with Bella. Pearl, get dressed and go and inform Sheriff Neiman. The rest of you, tidy yourselves and be ready for when the sheriff arrives.'

Reluctantly the girls dispersed, leaving Agatha, Loula and Tomas alone with the dead girl.

'Help me lift her on the bed.'

'Shouldn't we wait for the sheriff, ma'am, afore touching anything?'

'Just do as you're told!' Agatha snapped.

Tomas gripped the dead girl under her arms.

'Loula, help me with the feet,' Agatha ordered the sobbing girl.

Loula couldn't stop blubbing, but helped nevertheless. Together they lifted the body on to the bed.

'Turn her around, I have to get that cord off her neck.'

'Ma'am, I'm sure this ain't right, what you doing.'

'Tomas, trust me. You know who was in here with Bella last night.'

The big black man bowed his head and said nothing. Agatha was struggling with the cord.

'I can't budge this!'

Tomas pulled a clasp knife from his pocket and offered it up. Agatha took the knife and sawed at the cord. As the severed ends gave way the corpse gave a long sigh as if in relief at being released from the ligature. There was a scramble for the door as Loula and Tomas bolted. Agatha did not look up as her helpers deserted her. Concentrating on the task in hand, she pulled the cord free. As she worked, tears coursed down her cheeks.

'My poor Bella, you did not deserve this.'

She left the room and closed the door behind her. The necktie was safely tucked inside her pocket. Agatha went downstairs to the parlour where she found her helpers: Tomas shamefaced, while poor Loula looked terrified. Agatha instructed them on what to say should the sheriff wish to question them.

Mortimer Lecroy was in his office. Before leaving home that morning he had listened to his son's version of what had happened the previous evening. Though he suspected there was a lot that Verne was not telling him, he was inclined to believe his son's story.

'Then we all decided to go for a late night drink where my

friends assured me we could carouse all through the night.
When I woke up I was alone in a strange bed. I have no idea
how I got there or any recollection of what I did in the meantime. I presume I just fell asleep and my friends left me
sleeping.'

Verne made no mention of the dead whore.

'OK, you'd better go and lie down for a while. You look terrible.'

Mortimer Lecroy was mulling over his son's story and wondering what lay behind it. There was a something not quite
right about the whole thing.

'Damn the young blackguard, between drinking and
whoring, if he's not careful he'll get in real trouble.'

There was a tap on door and Sheriff Neiman entered.

'Ah, Garret, you wanted to see me.'

'Sure thing, Mortimer. Sorry to bother you.'

'No bother. Friends are never a bother. A drink – some
brandy perhaps?'

'Don't mind if I do.'

The sheriff was a slim man with an erect military bearing.
He settled into a large armchair and waited while his host
filled two glasses.

'Care for a cigar?'

There was another pause while cigars were produced and
lit.

'Cigars and brandy, the two pillars of civilization,' the
sheriff commented contentedly, puffing cigar smoke into the
room. 'You live well, Mortimer.'

'So-so, so-so. Now you've sampled my hospitality, perhaps
you'll tell me what brings you here.'

'Strange case came up this morning, Mortimer. A young
prostitute found murdered. When my men went to investigate
they asked the usual question. Who was last with the girl? The
madam would not tell them. She said she would only reveal

the identity to me.'

'And did she? I trust you'll make all efforts to find the culprit and bring him to boot. Even a prostitute has a right to justice.'

The sheriff did not answer immediately, but stared at his cigar while rolling it between finger and thumb.

'According to this lady, the murdered girl was strangled with a necktie. Before my men arrived on the scene she took this from around the girl's neck, which, as you are well aware, was unwarranted interference with evidence. She said there were witnesses as watched her do this.'

Mortimer Lecroy was beginning to feel uneasy as the sheriff narrated his tale. He waited for more.

'These witnesses are also aware of the identity of the man who spent the night with the murdered woman.'

Mortimer Lecroy was sitting very still. A slight tick began in one corner of his eye.

'You say she told you the man's name?'

Looking at his friend's face, the lawman felt sorry for him. Lecroy averted his gaze and stared down at his desk.

'She named your son, Verne. That's why she came to me. She wants to strike a deal. She claims her foremost concern is to protect the name of a valued client. The woman avers she'll keep quiet if we bury this case quickly. Another unsolved crime in the brothels of Callender.'

Lecroy blinked a few times and frowned at his colleague. There was a deep silence for several moments. Neiman smoked contentedly and supped his brandy. He was doing his old friend a favour. Handled correctly this sorry incident would be very profitable indeed.

'It's preposterous: Verne would never be implicated in such a crime. Why . . . why, he was with me all last night. It would be the word of a common whore against the word of . . . of me and my son.'

Lecroy uttered the last words in a hoarse whisper as if his voice was fading along with the colour in his face. His visitor nodded wisely.

'I think she anticipated that. That's why she removed the necktie. She has also taken the precaution of writing down sworn statements from members of her staff identifying Verne as the man who spent the night with the murdered whore.'

'Garret, what are we to do?'

'I've taken the precaution of putting the woman in a cell. In the meantime I've sent my deputies to arrest all the people in the brothel.'

14

Two deputies took Agatha from the jail across to the offices of Mortimer Lecroy. The banker was alone in his office when Agatha was brought in. She blinked nervously when she saw him. Agatha braced herself and waited for Lecroy to speak. Lecroy leaned back in his chair and looked up at the people standing nervously before him. His gaze slid over Agatha and rested momentarily on the deputies.

'Thank you, men. Wait outside.'

The door closed behind them and the two protagonists were left to appraise each other. Lecroy lounged back in his high-backed chair, eying up the very attractive young woman standing before him. Agatha straightened her shoulders and tried to look confident. Inside she was quaking. She understood that, through no fault of her own, her future was at stake. Just as Blain Larkin and his brother Moylan had crossed this powerful man and his son and lost out, now it was her turn. She was hoping she had a little more to bargain with than had the brothers.

'So madam, you think to incriminate an innocent man in this foul crime. You run a sinkhole of sin and wallow in filth, and in your degradation seek to pull others down with you. What have you to say for yourself?'

'Begging your pardon, Mr Lecroy, I am a humble businesswoman. I supply a service for men of particular tastes. They come from all walks of life. I do not question them about their motives or their background. They come to me melancholic and I send them away contented. At least that is my intention.'

Lecroy slammed his hand down on the desk, making Agatha flinch.

'You wallow in filth, madam. No matter how you dress up your trade, it is in truth a filthy business.'

'In that case, why was your son a regular customer? Is he tarred with the same filth you taint me with?'

'My son, never! Verne is a noble and god-fearing man. For whatever ends you are trying to ensnare him in your own devious schemes. I will not have it.'

Again he slapped the desk. Agatha did not flinch this time. There was a chair beside the desk. She walked forwards and seating herself, spent some moments smoothing down her skirts. Lecroy glared at her while she performed these actions. Agatha felt that in some small way she was asserting her independence when the banker made no objections to her taking a seat unbidden.

'Mr Lecroy, yesterday evening your son arrived at my establishment,' Agatha said calmly. 'He was drunk and almost incapable. Against my better judgement I allowed him to take one of my girls up to the rooms. And, by the way, your son is no stranger to my place. He has visited many times in the past. Next morning he left without paying for the services he received, which is not unusual. He has a habit of taking what he wants without payment.'

Lecroy sat with his eyes fixed on the woman in front of him, seemingly mesmerized by her words and behaviour.

'The girl he was with had been strangled with a distinctive gold-coloured necktie. I took that necktie and placed it in a package. Along with it I put the sworn statements of the people who witnessed all I did. They also attested as to your son's identity. A friend of mine now has that package in a safe place. If anything happens to me he will take it to a newspaper. After that it is in God's hands.'

'I do not for one minute believe anything of this fabrication,' Lecroy sneered. 'Coming from a woman who earns her living from sin, it would be doubtful if anyone else would believe it, either. I do admit such a story spread about could cause a certain amount of embarrassment. When enough mud is slung, some of it sticks. So in return for this package of invention of yours, I might be able to persuade Sheriff Neiman not to press charges.'

Agatha was starting to lose confidence in her ability to out-manoeuvre her opponent. After all, she was jousting with Mortimer Lecroy, with all the recourse of his immense wealth and influence behind him.

'Freedom for all my girls as well,' she ventured.

Lecroy's eyes narrowed, and Agatha grew afraid. She saw the thin, cruel lips twitch as he contemplated her. Suddenly he rose from his seat and came around the desk to stand in front of her. She tried not to shrink back as he faced her. His hand shot out and gripped her chin. Agatha could not help a small cry of fear. She felt the fingers dig into her throat and sensed the power in those hands. Her face was held up so she had to stare into the cold merciless eyes.

'You seek to bargain with me, woman. As well seek a bargain with Satan himself. I have the power of life and death over such as you. You are dirt beneath my feet that I scrape from the heels of my boots!

'Now here is what will happen. You and your harlots will be released. You will return here with this package that you have manufactured. Then, and only then, will I decide whether to let this matter drop or not. I decide what happens and does not happen in this town. Don't ever forget that!'

The last word was ground out along with drops of spittle that landed on Agatha's upturned face. She blinked rapidly and tried to pull her chin from that brutal grip.

'Understand!'

He shook her and the pain in her throat and jaw was unbearable. She tried to say yes, but her mouth was constricted and only an unintelligible moan emerged. Lecroy continued to jerk her head from side to side before releasing her. He returned to his seat behind the desk.

Agatha sat gasping and trembling. Lecroy's fierce man-handling had left her frightened and unsure. Instinctively she knew the battle was lost. She could not win against such a ruthless opponent.

'I will give you twenty-four hours. This time tomorrow you will report to me with this false evidence and place it in my hands here in this office. Give it to no one else. If you fail me in any of this, I will see you hang for the murder of that dead girl.'

15

The wagon lurched along the muddy road, the heavy load causing it to leave deep tracks that quickly filled with water. Rain was cascading on to the canvas like a thousand drumsticks hitting on the hide of a dead steer. It was inevitable that at some stage the wagon would pass over a cavernous pothole too deep for the wheels to cope with. The vehicle jerked, shuddered, and lurched to a stop. The driver yelled at the mules straining in the traces. His whip cracked again and again over the heads of the struggling animals.

'Get on there, you lazy sons of bitches!' he yelled, as rain sluiced off his hat brim and hammered cold rivets into his face. 'Goddamn you, move your lazy bitching hides!'

The mules strained valiantly in the traces but the wagon was stuck fast. The driver turned and pushed his face close to the front canvas.

'You'll have to bail out. We've hit a pothole.'

Cussing the rain, cussing the mules, cussing the wagon, cussing anything that came to mind, the man coiled his whip and placed it on the floor, then clambered down on the road. He sloshed through the mud to the rear of the wagon in time to see the canvas pulled open. One by one, three men crawled over the tailgate and joined him on the road. Two of the men from the wagon were hampered by chains on wrists and ankles.

'We'll try and push it clear,' the driver shouted. 'If that don't work we'll have to unload. Damn and blast!'

Within seconds the men from the wagon were soaked to

the skin. They hunched against the driving rain and leant their shivering bodies against the body of the wagon.

'I'll drive the mules on at the same time as you push,' the driver shouted. He sloshed forwards to the lead mules. 'When I call, you push your damndest!'

Seizing the reins on the leader he yelled out and threw his weight backwards, tugging on the traces. His passengers dug boots into the mud and pushed hard against the wagon.

Blain leaned his back against the tailgate and strained with all his strength in an effort to shift the solid bulk of the wagon. Beside him the smaller figure of Jephta worked with him. The youngster's shirtsleeve was dark with blood from the wound in his arm. Around the other side an older man gripped the spokes of the sunken wheel and heaved as the driver shouted.

For moments nothing happened. The driver was yelling encouragement to his comrades as he tugged on the reins. His team of mules brayed loudly in protest, but dug their hoofs in and leaned into the traces.

For the labourers, it felt as if they were pushing on the side of a barn. Rain pelted down mercilessly. The wagon moved slightly, and the boots and hoofs dug in deeper. Slowly but slowly the buried wheel turned, climbing the sides of the pothole.

'Harder!' the yell reached the soaked, straining men.

They called up reserves of strength they didn't know they possessed, and heaved mightily. Inch by inch the wagon moved, the wheels turning agonizingly slowly. Lungs bursting, breath coming in short bursts, they kept up the effort.

The driver was yelling at the mules. The mules were braying back in protest but did not let up hauling on their burden. The men at the back were locked solid against the wagon, limbs trembling, hearts bursting.

The wheel edged up, slipped, then inched forwards again.

Then all at once everything lurched forwards. Boots slipped in the mire as the wagon moved. Blain sat down on the road as his legs gave way beneath him. He did not care. He was soaked through anyway. Painfully he clambered to his feet. He turned and rested against the tailgate, his breath coming in short sobs. Jephta pulled himself up beside Blain and pushed his face against the canvas cover. They could not speak.

'Well done, fellas. We're on our way again. Sorry about that. I musta fallen asleep. Climb aboard for the Bourbon Express.'

The wagon rolled on, carrying stolen casks of bourbon and the two fugitives. This was the third day of travel. On the first night of their journey the young man driving the wagon had cleaned and bandaged the bullet wound in Jephta's arm. They dug a grave for their dead comrade, whom they had carried from the railhead. To Blain's surprise the young man conducted a respectable burial service, even to the extent of singing a hymn. They had stood around the pile of shovelled dirt and sung along with him. Afterwards they exchanged stories.

Blain told of his experiences at the hands of Lecroy, leaving out the part involving the brothel. Jephta refused to be drawn, saying he had killed a man, but giving no details.

'How the hell did you escape?'

They told of their fight in the train.

'Damn good thing you came along when you did. I reckon we were goners until you showed up. My name is Robert Sturdy. This here is Geoffrey Deese. I suppose you wonder what's going on, and by my reckoning you have a right to know. That was a shipment of whiskey bound for the gold-fields. We hijacked it. Whiskey is more valuable than gold out there.'

Blain asked where they were heading.

'There's a deserted town we use as a hideout. Ain't no one lives there excepting me and my men. Most of us are wanted by the law for one thing or another. So you'll feel at home there. It's a rough old place, but hell, it's somewhere to bed down.'

Before they could quiz him any further Sturdy suggested they have a go at removing their chains. He produced a hatchet from the wagon and hacked at the bracelets. Apart from blunting the axe nothing much was accomplished.

'I reckon you'll have to wear those irons awhile yet.'

Next day they were on the move again.

'If we're stopped, keep your weapons handy, but don't do anything rash,' Sturdy told them. 'Sometimes it's better to bluff your way than shoot your way out.'

It was still raining when they hit their destination. The sun was dying somewhere behind the rainclouds, creating an eerie half-light. In the abandoned buildings of the ghost town they could just make out empty windows and sagging doors. A lanky figure in oilskins stepped from a derelict store, a rifle held across his chest.

'Sturdy, it sure good to see you. How was the trip?'

'Good, only we lost Kersterson. Goddamn Pinkertons jumped us.'

They alighted in front of what had once been a hotel.

'I'm obliged to you fellas,' Sturdy told his passengers. 'At the end of the street is an old blacksmith's. You go on down and see if there is anything there to get those chains off.'

Inside a dilapidated livery they found a large anvil covered in rust. They rooted around and come up with a rusty chisel. It took a lot of hammering and bruised wrists and ankles but eventually they were free. Walking back up the street without their fetters it felt as if they were floating through the rain. When Sturdy saw them come in the hotel he came across.

'Come on you fellas, I owe you a drink.'

As they made their way to the bar Blain stumbled over a pair of legs.

'Goddamn, clumsy sonabitch!'

'Sorry,' Blain mumbled.

'I'll kill you.'

A pair of strong hands gripped Blain by his shirt and jerked him close. Instinctively the youngster struck out and smashed his attacker on the nose.

'Goddamn it!' the man roared pulling a knife.

Fearing for his life Blain brought up his knee into the man's crotch. There came a stream of curses and his attacker fell away. Suddenly a pair of brawny arms wrapped around him from behind.

'Ease up there, damn you,' a voice yelled in his ear.

A month or so ago Blain might have succumbed to the inevitable and allowed himself to be taken. But too much had happened to him since then. This was not the innocent youngster who only a short while ago had herded cattle. This Blain Larkin had already been responsible for the death of three men at least. He threw back his head, and the man holding him yelped as the back of the youngster's head bust his nose. Then Blain was falling forwards as his captor pushed him to the ground.

'Yippee, we got ourselves a ring-tailed gopher here!'

Blain was lying face down helpless when the attacker dropped on top of him.

'Kid, if I let you go will you promise not to hit anyone else?' a voice said in his ear.

'Eh,' Blain grunted trying to get his breath.

'I'll take that as a yeah.'

The grip on Blain loosened and the pressure on his back diminished. Warily he sat up and glared around him. A miscellany of grinning faces surrounded him. A hand came out towards him holding a bottle.

'Here kid, have a drink. You're wilder than a drunk polecat.'

16

It was an ignominious exit as the women were taken from the cells and dumped in the street. When they were arrested the deputies had driven up to the brothel and hustled them into a couple of wagons. They were taken to the jailhouse and shunted into the cells. Now that they were to be freed, they were pushed out into the street and had to find their own way back to the house from where they plied their trade.

'You're not men at all!' a buxom, fair-haired woman yelled, as they were being hustled into the street.

'If this is the law, then the law can kiss my ass!'

'Next time you come to the house you'd better bring your wife. She'd be more fun than you!'

Agatha rallied the women.

'Girls, we gotta make the best of things. Let's find a cab.'

Back at the brothel Agatha gathered the women in the parlour. She instructed Loula to fetch drinks for everyone.

'Anything they want. Mary, go in the kitchen and help Loula.'

Agatha waited until the drinks were served. Some of the females lit up tailor-made cigarettes, a habit that was catching on amongst women. Coffee, gin, brandy, whiskey and beer were among the beverages served up.

'Don't stint on the measures, Loula. We sure deserve some comforting after what we been through.'

It was a noisy gathering. The women sipped their drinks

and discussed the traumatic events that had dragged them from the reasonably secure life at the brothel into the turmoil of the last few days. At last Agatha stood before them and held up a hand for their attention.

'Sisters, this sordid affair has grave consequences for us. We are all aware who it was that took poor Bella's life the other night.'

This statement was greeted with muttered curses. The name 'Lecroy' was repeated a few times. Agatha waited until the noise abated.

'Today, I tried to make a deal with Mortimer Lecroy. The sad conclusion I came to is, that the rich and powerful have immunity from the law. Mortimer Lecroy made that very plain to me. In order to protect his son he forced me to make a deal.'

There was complete silence as the women in the room stared back at Agatha.

'He told me I had to leave Callender. If I don't go from here, Lecroy will see me charged with murder. As for anyone who worked here, he talked about conspiracy amongst you to pervert the course of justice, meaning anyone here might go to jail. He gave me twenty-four hours to get out of town.'

For a moment there was a shocked silence. Then the room filled with shrill female voices protesting the injustice of their treatment.

'What right has he. . . ?'

'Where is the justice. . . ?'

'Goddamn son of a bitch!'

Agatha held up her hand to still the flood of vitriol. It took a few moments for the noise to die down.

'I know it is unjust. People like Lecroy regard us as the dregs of society. They believe we have no rights. It has been our misfortune to be acquainted with the unpleasant truth about an eminent man in this godforsaken town. Therefore we must be silenced. We are banished. Either that or we go to prison. And as well, there is no guarantee the law won't hang us for the murder of poor Bella.'

There was a shocked silence at this last announcement. Then the babble started up again. Agatha was content to allow the chattering to run its course. She knew exactly what must be done.

Today, she had encountered a powerful and vengeful enemy. She had no doubt what course Mortimer Lecroy would follow. Once he had the evidence against his son in his hands he would take steps to silence Agatha. She knew her life in Callender was finished.

The trumped-up charge of murder might be carried to the extreme and she would be hanged, or – and she shuddered as she recalled the expression in Lecroy's eyes – he would find a more direct way of silencing her.

She was lying to the girls about the ultimatum from Lecroy that they had to leave town. She could run herself, but that would leave her girls vulnerable. Lecroy would hound them in an attempt to track her down. In order to protect the women she had to persuade them to quit along with her.

'We can catch a train going west. They say the miners are flooding into the goldfields. Can you imagine all those men away from their wives and girlfriends? And with gold to spend. Think how hungry they'll be for home comforts. We'll be back in business afore you can say "Mortimer Lecroy". Anyone as wants to stay on here is welcome. The rent's paid until the end of the month. But bear in mind what I said about the danger of staying.' She had to stem another outburst. 'While you make up your mind what you are going to do, I'm preparing to leave.'

There was much bustle as bags were packed and the women got ready to head for the railroad depot. Agatha was heading for the anonymity of the frontier, where she would lose herself. She was confident she could make a go of it, no matter where she landed. There were always lonely men hungry for female company. The goldfields were a honeypot and Agatha wanted to dip in and take her share of its riches. She was hoping that with the transfer of her business to another town it would throw Lecroy's hounds off the scent.

17

'You!'

Coming towards him with a snarl on his grubby face was Blackwell, the man with the knife whom Blain had tangled with the previous night. Blain was out in the town exploring the abandoned buildings when Blackwell accosted him. Reaching the youngster the bully pushed close. Blain tried to hold his breath so as not to inhale the rancid breath.

Blackwell was a big man with a burly frame. He was in his late forties, and grey stubble adorned a face that had more crevices than a mountain range. The mouth was mean and pinched. His expression was a habitual snarl, as if he hated everything and everyone.

Blain tried not to let anything of his fear and distaste show on his face. His eyes were almost crossed as he tried to focus on the repulsive face before him. Suddenly he felt a jolt of pain as Blackwell thrust the butt of the rifle he had been holding into Blain's crutch. The youngster grunted and bent forwards. Blackwell's forehead cracked into Blain's face. The youngster went down.

'That's for last night,' Blackwell yelled.

Blain was struggling to his feet but went down again as he was kicked in the ribs. As he lay there gasping in pain a figure came hurtling out from the hotel and launched itself at Blackwell. The big man turned too late as Jephta cannoned into him, and he was catapulted backwards. The breath was knocked out of Blackwell as he hit the ground. Jephta thrust the barrel of his six-gun inside the mouth of the man underneath him.

'I took this gun off a lawman,' Jephta yelled. 'He's dead now. I'm sure he would rest easier in his grave to know his pistol was about to blow a goddamn son of a bitch of an outlaw to kingdom come.'

Blackwell's eyes were wide with terror. Blain was climbing painfully to his feet. He caught a movement out of the corner of his eye. Creeping towards Jephta was Jordan Willer.

Somewhat younger than his partner, Willer had the lean, drawn look of a man with a grudge against life in general. His rifle was raised ready to strike the youth who had impulsively leapt to Blain's rescue.

'Jephta,' Blain shouted and lurched forward.

Blain went in low and crashed into the man's ribs. Willer did not have time to react. He had the rifle by the barrel and his whole attention was on Jephta. As Willer went down Blain made a grab for his rifle. They fell to the ground with both men holding on to the weapon.

Blain pushed down on the rifle and the barrel came to rest just above Willer's neck. The outlaw yelled curses as he desperately tried to keep the steel from crushing his windpipe. Blain kept up the pressure and the two men strained for an advantage.

'Damn you,' Willer yelled. 'Someone get this lunatic off me!'

Men were gathering around to watch the fight. No one moved to help.

'Come on, you coward!' Jephta yelled as he sat astride his captive. 'Give me a reason why I shouldn't blow you to kingdom come.'

There was an insane glow about the youth's eyes. Blackwell stopped struggling and stared in terror at his tormentor. Beside them the struggle between Blain and Willer continued. Blain had the advantage for he was on top and was able to use his weight to bear down on the rifle. Willer had enough strength to keep the rifle barrel from crushing his throat, but the strain was taking its toll. Sweat beaded on his forehead and his arms trembled with the effort.

Blain was tiring, too. The tension of bearing down on the rifle was beginning to tell. It was mostly his weight that was keeping the weapon where it was. In effect it was a stalemate, with neither of the men able to gain advantage. Locked in their silent struggle they grunted and strained and snarled at each other.

'Stop, damn you!' a voice shouted out.

Blain looked up, and seeing Robert Sturdy striding towards them, released his hold on the rifle. The youngster rolled off his victim and clambered to his feet. Willer, now in sole possession of the rifle, drove it hard and brutally into Blain's midriff. With a grunt the youngster folded over and went down on his knees, his hands grasping his middle.

Before Sturdy could intervene, Willer smashed the butt of the weapon into the side of Blain's head. The youngster sprawled sideways and remained ominously still. Willer, having disposed of his opponent, turned his attention to Jephta. Sturdy saw the murderous intention in the man's eyes.

'Willer,' he yelled, 'stay where you are!'

He might as well have whistled a tune for all the notice Willer took. The outlaw swung the rife. Out of the corner of his eye Jephta saw the rifle coming. He flung himself to one side and the rifle missed, hitting Blackwell on the knee instead. The bully grabbed his injury and roared with pain. Lying in the dirt, Jephta aimed his revolver at Willer.

'Try that again and you're dead,' Jephta yelled.

Willer hesitated. It was enough time for Sturdy to step in front of him.

'That's enough, Willer. This stops now.'

For a moment Sturdy thought the enraged man was going to attack him.

'Get out of my way. I'm gonna brain that bastard.'

'Willer, step back out of my face!'

Sturdy had his hand on his holstered Colt. The two men stood eyeball to eyeball for what seemed ages. Willer was sweating, his face a bright crimson. He was breathing heavily. Sturdy could smell the rancid stench of body odour coming off the man, but he held his gaze steady. He readied himself to pull his gun at the first hint Willer might be crazed enough to attack him.

'Willer!' Sturdy's voice was low and threatening.

It was touch and go, but the crazed man slowly lowered the rifle, never taking his eyes from Sturdy. Sturdy glanced around to see Blackwell sitting up, massaging his injured leg, an ugly scowl on his face.

'Those goddamn kids are a pair of crazed animals,' he snarled, as he heaved himself to his feet. 'Going around attacking people.' He was glaring at Sturdy, tenderly feeling his mouth. There was a faint smear of blood on his chin. 'You should never have brought those hellions here. They're nothing but trouble.'

'They're here under my protection,' Sturdy growled. 'And I owe them my life.'

Blackwell glared back at him, and the outlaw chief saw the hatred in the man's eyes. Sturdy stayed where he was, waiting. It was Blackwell who dropped his eyes.

The bullies turned away and slouched down the street. Sturdy looked down at the youngster lying in the dirt. Blain had not recovered from the blow on the head. Sturdy could see blood trickling down his face.

'Someone help me carry Larkin inside.'

Two men volunteered to carry the unconscious Blain, with Jephta tagging along. They carried him into the hotel and up to one of the bedrooms. Jephta hovered uncertainly with a worried look until Sturdy buttonholed him.

'Right Jephta, what the hell was going on back there?'

'Blackwell attacked Blain. So I jumped him. We were doing all right until you came along.'

'I'm relieved you didn't have to shoot Blackwell. He's a mean bastard, but a good man with explosives. He can blow a safe in less time than you take to open a can of beans.'

Jephta took out the gun and grinned at the other man.

'I couldn't have shot him anyways – it's empty. I used the last bullet on that lawman back at the railhead.'

Sturdy chuckled. To have held Blackwell and his repulsive pal at bay with an empty pistol was farcical to say the least. The more he thought about it, the more he admired these youngsters who leapt into troubled waters with no thought of the consequences for themselves.

'Will Blain be all right?' Jephta asked.

'What?'

Sturdy had been in another plane altogether when Jephta asked the question. He had been thinking of the stolen bourbon. He had contacts in his home town of Grantham where he thought to sell the contraband. Grantham was where his sister and parents lived. He was thinking it was time to go back home and mix a little pleasure with business. With a start he came back to the present and answered Jephta's question regarding Bain.

'Yeah, I guess. He's young and fit. But watch out for

Blackwell and Willer. They're a mean pair, and they'll not like being bested. Watch your back. And tell Blain to do the same.'

18

When Verne Lecroy made the move to Crow's Butte where he was to expand the family banking business he rented an imposing red brick town house. His buddies, Tex Plant and James Hedger who were to guide and protect him, also accompanied him.

'The first thing I am going to do is take a bath. See if you can get a fire going and heat some water. I'm going into town to find out where the best places are for the pursuit of pleasure. When I return I'll have my bath and then we'll sally forth and sample the fleshpots of Crow's Butte.'

That evening the three gallants readied themselves to venture out and visit the saloons and bordellos.

'What you got planned for us tonight, Verne?'

'I was told Clinton's Hotel serve a decent supper. I've booked a table. Once we've dined we can start the evening proper. I'm told there is a new brothel opened. We'll visit that as well.'

Lecroy ordered a cab to take them into town. It was hot and stuffy in the mining town that evening. The streets were thronged with drunk and rowdy miners. The saloons were bursting with noise and music.

They drove through the streets and were intrigued at the sights and sounds that greeted them. On every available open space clusters of tents had sprung up like mushrooms in a paddock. What at first they had assumed were fireworks turned out to be gunshots. The newcomers saw miners brawling and drunks reeling and falling down and being sick.

'Good lord, is this what the country has become,' exclaimed Verne. 'They must have dredged the sewers to gather up such scum.'

'The gold strikes have attracted the dregs of society. Fellas that couldn't make it in any other profession have come out here hoping to make good.'

'Yeah, I reckon every varmint and hellion and his uncle have descended on Crow's Butte.'

'The thought of striking it rich in the gold diggings does something to a man, I reckon. It fries his brain so he don't have to think none.'

'As long as they keep digging it up and depositing it in my bank then I'll cheer them on.'

The night was well established by the time the three men staggered out from the Drum and Trumpet, a seedy saloon that was rowdy and smoke-filled and crowded with drunken revellers. At one point a miner, well in his cups, staggered up to Lecroy.

'I hate tenderfoots. I'm gonna shoot as many tenderfoots as come within range of my gun.'

Verne eyed the man with some distain.

'You couldn't shoot your foot if someone held the gun for you.'

The man had a Remington revolver tucked in a pocket. He tugged at it but the hammer snagged on the material of his coat. Plant pulled his own revolver and shoved it in the man's face.

'How's about I shoot you in the eye and let some light in your brain?' the gunman asked him.

The drunk tried to focus on the gun in Plant's hand. He let go his own weapon and suddenly lost interest in the man he wanted to shoot. After that there was no more trouble. The three men drank in peace and left the saloon after a heavy drinking session. The bartender had given them directions to the new brothel. They hailed a hack to take them.

The whole town was in turmoil. They passed a cab over-turned and on fire. Men were dancing around the blaze in a drunken frenzy. It was as if the miners were on one drunken orgy. At length they pulled up at a two-story brick building.

'This is it,' the driver called.

Hedger hammered on the door. Across the road a fight broke out. Not far away shots were heard.

'Goddamn it, this is the way to live!'

Verne grinned at his companions. The door opened and a big black man stood framed in the doorway.

'Well, I'll be blowed!' Verne exclaimed. 'What have we here? If it ain't Tomas, late of Callender.'

The black man stared out at Verne and his companions, a look of stunned disbelief on his face. He tried to slam the door. Tex Plant was too quick for him. His boot was in the way. James Hedger flung himself behind Plant and they forced the black man to give way. All three of the newcomers crowded into the dimly lit hallway.

'Tomas,' Verne chided, 'what way is that to treat an old friend?'

19

Tomas was visibly shaking as he looked at the three men crowded into the hallway.

'Master Lecroy, I sure didn't recognize you just then.'

The black man turned his head and opened his mouth as if to shout to someone in the house. Hedger punched him hard on the chin and the black man's mouth slammed shut. He staggered back and Hedger pulled an Adams revolver and pushed it in his face. Tomas went very still.

'I done want no trouble,' he mumbled. 'Nosiree, I ain't wantin' no trouble.'

'What's going on here, Tomas? Is that cow Agatha with you?'

'Agatha, which one is that, sir?'

Hedger slashed the barrel of his revolver into the side of Tomas's head. He gave a little mew of pain and cowered back from the intruders. Big as he was, he was no match for the three thugs. There was nowhere for the houseman to go. The men had him crowded against the wall. A door led into the interior of the house, but that was closed.

'Listen, you piece of dung,' Hedger snarled, 'when Mister Lecroy asks a question you answer with respect. I ain't shot me anyone in a while and I'm sure aching to put a bullet in that black hide of yours.'

Blood trickled down Tomas's face. He kept very still, not wanting to provoke the men into more violence.

'Yes sir, Mister Lecroy, I tell you what you wants to know,' he said in a trembling voice. 'Miss Agatha she inside. She be glad to see you.'

'I'm sure. Now Tomas, we'll all go inside. You lead the way. Hedger, keep that pistol on him. He makes a wrong move put a bullet in him, but try not to kill him. I want him to suffer if he tries to trick us.'

Hedger opened the inner door and the little procession filed inside. A staircase led upstairs. Tomas ignored the stairs and led them further inside. He stopped at a door and turned to look over his shoulder.

'This is the parlour. Miss Agatha she inside.'

'Hedger, you go first. Hide that pistol. Tomas next, with me behind and then Plant. Shoot anyone as gives trouble. With all the guns going off outside no one will take any notice. Plant, you shoot Tomas if he looks like he might give trouble. Let's go!'

Agatha was sitting at ease on a padded armchair sipping a glass of brandy. Two scantily dressed young women were lounging on a couch. There were more couches lined up around the room. The floor was carpeted and the parlour was illuminated by oil lamps mounted on the walls of the room. All the women looked up as Tomas entered with Hedger.

Agatha smiled a welcome and set her glass on a small polished table. She was about to rise when she recognized the man behind Hedger. Her hand flew to her mouth and she gave a small cry. She stayed where she was, unable to rise as fear crept over her like an incoming tide.

'Agatha!' Lecroy was grinning widely as he greeted the madam. 'What a lovely surprise.'

Using his pistol Plant prodded Tomas forward. The black man stumbled further into the room, his head hanging down, unable to look at his mistress.

'Mister Lecroy,' Agatha stuttered, 'what a pleasant surprise. It is good to see old friends again. What brings you to Crow's Butte?'

Verne walked slowly forward until he was standing directly in front of Agatha. She had been shocked into immobility once she recognized her visitors. There were shades of terror in her eyes as she gazed up at the man who had caused her so much trouble.

'My father was upset when you left without as much as a goodbye,' Verne said. 'He will be pleased when I tell him I have found you. He has men looking for you. I suppose they would have found you eventually.'

'I want no trouble,' Agatha said shakily. 'I kept my mouth shut. You have nothing to fear from me.'

Verne reached out and gently ran a finger along Agatha's cheek. She could not help flinching.

'I never feared you, Agatha. I always admired you.'

Verne transferred his hand to her head and stroked her hair. Agatha had long hair the colour of spun gold. She had lost weight since her easy days back in Callender. Now she had a svelte figure encased in a tight-fitting green silk gown. She looked extremely desirable and very, very scared.

The two young women, sensing something was not quite right, stayed very still and quiet. Hedger had walked to the far side of the room and was grinning as he watched his boss tease the frightened woman. Plant kept his pistol on Tomas, who stood trembling as he anticipated the trouble that would surely come from the callous trio.

Tomas was a big man and immensely strong, but he knew the reputation of these men. He knew very well they would shoot him without a thought. So he stood and trembled and feared for his mistress.

Lecroy looked around the room, his gaze finally lighting on the two frightened women quietly watching him.

'This is very cosy. Three eager females and three willing men.'

He let his gaze linger on Tomas. The black man was beginning to sweat, giving off the smell of fear.

'It seems to me you are the odd one out, Tomas. There is no woman for you and we sure aren't sharing. Lie on the floor. Hedger, find something to tie him up.'

'Done kill me, Mr Lecroy,' Tomas pleaded. 'Remember I saved your life on that day that young fella was gonna shoot you. I stopped him then. I would do it again if'n I got the chance.'

Verne ignored him. Plant hit Tomas on the back of the head with his pistol. The big man sank to his knees moaning as he feared the worst.

'Lie down like the man told you!' Plant snarled.

Tomas flopped to the carpet and lay trembling. Hedger ripped ornamental rope curtain ties from their moorings, and coming across quickly trussed the houseman. With Tomas helpless, Verne turned once more to Agatha.

'Now my dear, you and I are going to get reacquainted.'

His hand snaked out and slapped her hard across the face. Agatha's head rocked back. She turned her shocked face up to him. A thin trickle of blood leaked from her nose. Verne did not turn as his men pounced on the other two females. He was grinning down at the terrified woman.

'I'll teach you to run away. Nobody causes me trouble and gets away with it. When I've finished this lesson, I'm going to send you back to Callender. Pa reckons you're guilty of murdering a poor woman who worked for you. Then there's the matter of trying to blackmail him. Pa, he's just aching to see you hanged.'

20

Agatha was lying on the carpet, her face bruised and bloody; her eyes swollen and almost closed. Angry red wheals covered her body, crisscrossing her stomach and thighs.

The two females, unfortunate enough to have been caught in the parlour along with their mistress, huddled together on a couch sobbing quietly. Near them on the floor lay Tomas, his hands tied behind his back, eyes closed against the madness going on inside the room.

Verne Lecroy was swigging from a brandy bottle. Dangling from his free hand was a length of the ornamental rope used to tie back the heavy velvet curtains.

'Get dressed, you whore,' he growled at Agatha. 'It's time for a little trip. Hedger, see if that hack is still outside.'

'I can't see him waiting this length of time without a retainer,' Hedger grumbled as he pulled on his clothes. 'I'll probably have to go looking for one.'

'Well, bloody go looking!' snarled his boss. 'What the hell do I pay you for?'

'OK, OK. I'm going as soon as I get dressed.'

Lecroy scowled and put the brandy bottle to his mouth.

'Goddamn bitch is more trouble than she's worth. Maybe a bullet in the head might save us a lot of trouble,' he grumbled.

'You'd havta do the same to all these people in the room.'

Hedger was leisurely buttoning his shirt as he made this contribution.

'Hell, they're only little people,' Lecroy grunted. 'Way

down at the bottom of the pile. No one would miss them.'

'I think four deaths in one night might be hard to explain. Let's just stick with the original plan. We take the madam and deliver her to the local law. They'll ship her back to Callender.'

'Hedger, when I need your advice I'll ask for it. Right now just shut your mouth and do what I tell you.' Lecroy turned to Agatha. 'You bitch, hurry up with your clothes before I decide to have another go at you with this rope.'

Hedger scurried from the room before his boss turned his ire on him. Agatha gathered her clothing. Tugging on the garments she winced as the fabric rubbed her raw and bleeding skin. Her trembling fingers struggled with the fastenings on her dress. There was a commotion at the street door and raised voices.

'You can't come in here,' Hedger was shouting. 'This is a private house.'

'Private my ass! We know the girls here. We come for a bit of funning.'

'Come back tomorrow night, or better still come back in an hour. Everything will be free then.'

'Hey fellas, this guy's bumming us. What's going on here? There was never anything free in this hellhole of a town.'

'Sure thing, Marvin, they'd charge for the air we breathe only it's so foul nobody would pay.'

There were hoots of laughter at this, then sounds of a struggle.

'Watch out fellas, he's got a gun!'

'Shoot the bastard,' someone called.

A shot rang out. Verne strode to the parlour door and wrenched it open. Tex Plant quickly followed.

'Hedger, what the hell's going on?' Verne called as he edged into the hallway.

'These guys want in,' Hedger answered.

'You men,' Verne shouted, 'put up your weapons. And back off.'

Left unguarded, Agatha dropped to her knees beside Tomas and fumbled with the rope around his wrists.

'Hush,' she whispered as the black man opened his eyes and stared up at her. 'We'll get out the back way and make a run for it.'

She broke a nail in the effort but managed to undo the knots. Tomas stood up and glanced fearfully at the door.

'Grab your clothing,' Agatha whispered to the two women watching her with frightened eyes. 'No time to get dressed. Follow me out the back.'

Another shot rang out. The escapees flinched as the sound tore at already shredded nerves.

'The next shot will be in someone's skull instead of over your heads,' Lecroy called. 'We got an injured woman inside. We need to get her to a doctor. If you galoots back off and let us take her out, you can come on in as soon as we leave.'

There was more arguing back and forth.

'All right, but hurry it up,' someone growled. 'We sure are anxious to get to them there fillies.'

'Hedger, bring out the woman. You men keep clear of the doorway. I want no more trouble. The place is yours as soon as we're out in the street.'

Inside the parlour Agatha had pulled aside a curtain to reveal a door. She was struggling to open it when she heard Verne ordering Hedger to fetch her out.

'Goddamn door open,' she hissed.

The door was stiff with not being used overmuch. Tomas was coming to help when he heard the footsteps outside. He turned and ran across the room. Hedger was curling his hand around the door and pushing it open when Tomas hit it with his shoulder.

The door jarred closed with a solid thud. Hedger

screamed. Tomas was staring with horror at the fingers jutting from the closed door. The screaming went on. Verne was shouting. Footsteps were running along the hallway. In spite of his terror Tomas kept his bulk firmly wedged against the solid door.

'What the hell's happening, Hedger?'

With his fingers clamped in the door and blood spilling from the crushed members Hedger could only continue to howl and blubber. Verne pounded on the door and rattled the handle.

'Open this goddamn door,' he bawled.

Shaking in terror Tomas leaned hard against the door. He glanced over at Agatha. She was still cursing and kicking at the other door.

The noise from the hallway ceased. Tomas put his ear to the wood panel in an effort to hear what his enemies were up to. The shot that was fired through the door hit him in the throat. The big man's eyes opened wide. He gave an odd bubbling cry. Another shot splintered a panel but missed Tomas. He put his hand to his throat to stem the blood pouring from the wound. Slowly he slid down the door. His eyes were fixed wide and full of pain as he stared across at Agatha. She turned around at the sound of the shot and with an expression of horror as she saw the blood on Tomas's neck.

'Tomas,' she moaned.

He shook his head at her and raised his hand as if in farewell then fell sideways, his bulky body effectively making a barricade it would be difficult to shift. More shots ploughed through the panelled door, the explosions sounding loud and menacing inside the room.

It was the turn of the two partially clad females to scream as they saw Tomas collapse with the blood spilling from his wound. The pounding on the door started up again along with the shouting. Agatha threw her shoulder hard at the jammed door and of a sudden it gave way. She almost fell through.

'Come on!' she hissed at the women.

Without waiting to see if they followed, she was through the door and out into the yard. Behind her, more shots rang out as the men in the hall took out their frustration on the door and decided to shoot it to pieces. Agatha ran into the night, heedless of where she was going, her body hurting and her heart grieving for Tomas.

'Damn you Verne Lecroy!' she sobbed. 'You have wrecked my life and killed some good people that never did you no harm. If I was a man I would take a gun and shoot you down like the mad dog you are.'

Through back alleys she fled, having to evade clutching hands and shouted curses as drunken revellers tried to persuade her to join them. But Agatha was running. She was fleeing the clutches of Verne Lecroy. She knew what she was fleeing from, but she had no idea where she was fleeing to.

21

Emelie Sturdy stood outside the large clapboard house, a bible clutched in her hands, and sang with deep fervour. Standing beside Emelie, her mother was singing just as lustily. Her father stood with them and led the singing with a fine deep voice.

With broken heart and contrite sigh,
A trembling sinner, Lord I cry;

Thy pardoning grace is rich and free:
O God be merciful to me!

Standing straight and firm, Emelie was almost as tall as her father. She had full, sensuous lips and a ready smile. Her hair formed a red halo around her fine-looking face. Clear hazel eyes stared out at the world. A navy blue woollen cloak, pulled high against the evening chill, hid her full womanly figure.

A window opened on the second floor. A woman poked her head out.

'Cease that caterwauling at once, you God-botherers,' a strident female voice cried out. 'You are upsetting my girls, not to mention my clientèle.'

Reverend Sturdy held up a hand and the singing faded.

'Madam, the Lord has called us to his work. We are here to bring the forgiveness and mercy of the good Lord to you and your poor misguided girls. Let compassion enter your soul. Cease this wicked work you indulge in. Close down this house of sin and repent.'

'God's curse on you! You're nothing but a crowd of hypocrites. I've seen you in here, Reverend Sturdy, wrestling with my girls. What does your pox-ridden wife think of that? She's nought but a dried-up prune, and you have to come here and cavort with my girls. Come on up and I'll give you a free one. Then maybe you'll go home and stop bothering honest working women.'

'I forgive you for this slander. I know it is Satan that puts these untruths in your mouth. Reject the Prince of Evil. Repent and your sins will be forgiven.'

There was a sudden movement at the window. Fortunately for the proselytizers, the woman was finding it difficult to retain her balance and empty her pail at the same time. The deluge cascaded to the steps and splashed the parson's shoes instead of his head, as was intended. Emelie stepped back

82

instinctively, as did the rest of the little company.

'Ooh, disgusting,' a stout woman in a hooded grey cloak exclaimed.

Emelie felt faint as the stench grew. She dug out her handkerchief and pressed it to her nose. She thought she might pass out, and swayed unsteadily. Beside her, the woman in the grey cloak reached out a hand to steady the girl.

'What filthy behaviour,' she called. 'Have you no respect for a man of the cloth? Reverend Sturdy is here to save your souls, and you abuse him by emptying your night soil on him.'

Reverend Sturdy was an emaciated scarecrow of a man. Dressed in black as befitting a man of God, bony wrists protruded from his shabby jacket. His gaunt face was partly covered with untidy sparse whiskers. Beside him, his wife, Gertrude, was looking with some horror at the foul mess on the pavement. She had been a handsome woman at one time, but now her face was lined and careworn.

'Come Howell,' she pleaded with her husband. 'We must go now before more abuse is poured upon us.'

That skeletal hand rose in the air as Reverend Sturdy spoke out.

'So too are all servants of the Lord abused. Did not Isaiah warn us that the ungodly would reject the Word of God? He is despised and rejected of men; a man of sorrows and acquainted with grief, and we hid our faces from him; he was despised and we esteemed him not.'

In the end Mrs Sturdy prevailed and persuaded her husband to call it a night and return home. The preacher turned to his little band of missionaries. It was composed entirely of women, numbering half a dozen. Plainly dressed, they looked up at the preacher with a mixture of solidarity and respect.

'Dear brethren, it is your good faith and staunch support that sustains me to go on preaching the Word to our fallen sisters. The hand of the Lord has touched you. Take heart in the knowledge that you occupy a special place in the heavenly kingdom. You are the vigilant children of the Lord. God does love a sinner, but he loves an apostle with a special and singular attentiveness.'

On this note Reverend Sturdy told his followers to depart to their homes with a clear conscience. They had sought to bring enlightenment to sinners. They had broadcast the seed. Some would fall among nettles and thorns and some on stony ground, but surely some would fall on fertile ground.

Grantham was a growing town. Whorehouses had sprung up within its boundaries. The influx of men hoping to dig out the rich ores of the surrounding hills had attracted women who made a living from the cravings of lustful men.

When Reverend Sturdy had begun his mission for fallen women he had thoughts of providing a house for them to take refuge from the brothels. He had broached the possibility of opening his own small home to the fallen doves. His wife, usually an uncomplaining accomplice of his religious excesses, had drawn the line at that.

'Howell, we have our daughter's welfare to consider. I will not expose her to the vulgarities of these women. One cannot wallow in the sty without being contaminated. You'll just have to go on seeking a suitable residence for these unfortunate creatures. I'm sure the Lord will provide.'

The little congregation made their way through the streets. Even at that late hour the thoroughfares were teeming with life. As they progressed, the devotees trailed off to their homes until only the Reverend Sturdy and his wife and daughter were left.

The Sturdy home was a small brick building in a row of such houses. Neat gardens with picket fences fronted the humble homes. As they turned into the street the footsteps of the three missionaries slowed as they saw three men in front of their home. They were used to seeing such men, usually drunk and swaggering about the streets of Grantham, cursing and calling out insults to anyone who happened to cross their paths.

'See Howell,' Mrs Sturdy hissed, 'word must have got about that you shelter fallen women in our home. It looks as if those rascals have come to our street with sinful intentions. It is utterly shameful and vexatious. You better speak sternly to them and send them on their way. Emelie and I will wait here while you do your duty. And spare not their feelings. They are shameless in their desire for sinning.'

'Yes dear, I shall read a passage of the good book to them.'

'Emelie!' Mrs Sturdy shrieked.

The reason for the exclamation was the sight of her daughter running along the street towards their home.

'Oh my God! Preserve my daughter from her madness,' she wailed and would have fainted but for the supporting arm of her husband.

Then she did faint, for she saw her daughter flinging herself into the arms of one of the men and hugging him with unalloyed abandon.

22

The atmosphere in the Sturdy household changed dramatically with the homecoming of their son. Mrs Sturdy became animated and lively, fussing around Robert as if he were the most important person in her little world. The Reverend Sturdy was stiff and formal with his son and it was easy to sense an air of tension between the two men. It was Emelie who changed most of all.

Generally a shy, retiring young woman, used to keeping a modest behaviour as befits the daughter of a preacher, she became energized with the arrival of her beloved brother. She clung to his arm and watched his face with undue fondness. Robert introduced his companions.

'These are my guardian angels, Blain Larkin and Jephta Owens.'

There were smiles and polite handshakes all round.

'Your guardian angels, Robert, how so?'

'These men saved my life.'

Blain was hardly taking in the conversation as Robert Sturdy sang the praises of himself and Jephta. He was gazing with unadulterated admiration at Emelie. Never in his life could he have imagined anyone so beautiful. Her young face was animated as she hovered around Robert. The excitement of having her brother home had given her an added lustre. Blain felt something ignite deep inside. When he was introduced to her and his hand touched hers, an intense feeling of tenderness flooded through him.

'Pl . . . pl . . . pleased to meet you,' he stammered.

Emelie saw the sudden longing in his eyes as their hands met. A sensation in the pit of her stomach lurched into life and momentarily glowed in her clear hazel eyes. Unaccustomed sentiments flared, as the ardent blue eyes of the stranger gazed at her with out-and-out admiration. The strength of feeling suddenly unleashed within her frightened her not a little. The two youngsters were like that for only seconds, yet it seemed as if they gazed at each other for a long time.

'Emelie! What is the matter with that girl?'

It took some effort to pull her hand away and drop her gaze from those exceptional blue eyes as Emelie realized her mother was speaking to her.

'Mother?' she asked, acutely aware of the presence of their young visitor.

'Dear child, you'll have to stop daydreaming and pay attention. I said, run along to Mr Thornberry and ask him if he can spare a chicken and if he would have apples enough to make a pie for your brother and his friends. Would that be too much to ask? We have sufficient potatoes and greens for the supper. I'll do roast chicken.'

'Mother,' Robert protested, 'there's no need to go to any trouble. A bit of cornpone and a drink would be adequate.'

He missed the look Jephta gave him. They hadn't eaten since leaving the derelict town that morning, and the youngster, though slight of build, had a voracious appetite. But Mrs Sturdy was determined to welcome her son and his companions with a proper cooked meal, and Emelie was told to carry out her mother's instructions and fetch the extra fodder.

'Perhaps I should go with her,' Blain offered gallantly. 'The streets seem a bit rowdy as we walked here. I could help carry the things,' he finished lamely.

'Most gentlemanly of you, Blain.'

Robert was grinning hugely as he slapped the youth on the back. He turned to his mother and wrapped his arms around her.

'Mother, I'm sure it's your prayers that have kept me safe up until now, so you can put in a word in to the Good Lord for Jephta and Blain here while you're at it.'

Mrs Sturdy, unused to tokens of affection, looked embarrassed as her son held her. She tried to look annoyed but could not quite manage it. A slight flush started in her cheeks as she gazed fondly up at her big son.

'Go on with you,' she chided. 'You always were one for sweet-talking.'

While this banter was going on, Emelie put on her cloak and picked up a basket. As no one had objected to his tagging along, Blain held the door for her and they went quickly outside.

'Don't dally, Emelie. Go as quick as you can,' Mrs Sturdy called, as the door closed behind them.

The youngsters walked side by side, intensely aware of each other. Emelie was eighteen, almost two years older than Blain. She had no experience of talking to boys. Most of her socializing was spent with the older members of her congregation. She was struck dumb in the presence of this youngster who had lit a spark within her when he had looked at her with his intense blue eyes. She walked in silence with downcast eyes. Blain walked beside her, equally dumb in the presence of this goddess. He strained to think of something to say but his brain remained a blank.

'How . . . how far is it?' he said at last, desperate to break the strained silence between them.

She looked at him from beneath long pale eyelashes and the flawless beauty of her features made him catch his breath.

'Far! How far is what?'

'The store, is it far into town?'

'Oh no, you mean for us to fetch the vittles!' She suddenly laughed and it was the trilling of birdsong in his ears. 'No, Mr Thornberry is a parishioner who has a few acres and keeps cows and chickens and grows vegetables. He is a dear old chap. I've known him since I was a little girl.'

Emelie was pleased to talk about something. The silence had made her anxious. She was worried their young visitor might think her dull.

'Mr Thornberry's wife died last year, and he is a lonely old soul.'

That subject exhausted, they walked in silence again. But the ice was broken and the silence seemed more companionable.

'How did you meet Robert?' Emelie asked at last.

Blain hesitated before replying. 'It was when I was running from some people. I got mixed up in a duel. . . .'

Those hazel eyes turned their full gaze on him and Blain knew he could not tell her the whole truth.

'A duel! My goodness, but you're so young! Did . . . did you kill . . . hurt anyone?'

'I wounded someone, but didn't kill him. I was put in prison for it.'

'How awful! Were you pardoned?'

'No, I escaped.'

She was watching at him with an animated expression on her face. The young man her brother had brought home was taking on a romantic, heroic image in her mind.

'Was that before you met Robert?'

'That was when I was on the run. There were a couple of fellas had the drop on Robert. I . . . we, I mean, Jephta and me, we jumped them and rescued Robert.'

'That is the most romantic tale I have ever listened to. Gosh, you're like a knight of the olden days. Going round duelling and rescuing people in distress!'

The road disappeared from beneath Blain's feet. He trod on clouds and walked in a kind of daze beside the most beautiful woman in the world. Suddenly all the terrible things that had occurred in the past months fitted into place. There had been a plan behind it all. That plan had led him to this point in his life. Nothing in his past mattered. What mattered was the here and now. Walking beside this divine creature was his reward after enduring the hardships of the past few months. Blain Larkin was madly and gloriously in love. He walked on air and the world had taken on a roseate glow.

23

On Mrs Sturdy's insistence the three stayed the night. Robert was given his old room, which his mother had kept just as he had left it. Blain and Jephta had to sleep in the living room. They were plied with blankets and pillows to make up beds.

'Are you sure you're going to be all right?'

Mrs Sturdy fluttered round the boys like a mother hen. Her daughter hovered around trying her best not to look at Blain and not succeeding very well. Blain, acutely aware of her presence, was at his most charming with Mrs Sturdy.

'Ma'am, this is luxury compared to the places where we have to sleep at times,' Blain reassured her.

He thought it prudent not to regale her with images of the foul habits of the men in Robert's gang. The outlaws seemed not to have heard of the cleansing properties of soap and water. Blain had found it hard to adjust to the sordid living he was forced to endure in the deserted township. It was no wonder Robert insisted they call at a bathhouse on arrival at Grantham and have their clothes steamed while they luxuriated in their first bath for months. Jephta was the only one to object.

'Hell, I don't need no bath. It ain't natural, so much washing. My pa reckoned it weakens the body.'

'When did you last have a bath?'

Sturdy looked amused as he asked the question.

'Huh, I don't recollect.'

'Listen to me, Owens. I am taking you to visit my family. So either you come into this bathhouse now, where you will wash all of your body, and have your clothes deloused, or you will be abandoned here to fend for yourself!'

Now that he had met Emelie, Blain was doubly glad her brother had insisted on the bathing. Reposing in the same house as the celestial Emelie, Blain was imagining how she would react if he crept up to her bedroom and made his feelings known to her. Immediately he felt ashamed of his speculations. She's not like that, he told himself. Emelie was a respectable girl and a preacher's daughter. To distract himself, he turned his attention to his companion.

'Jephta, are you sleeping?'

'Nah, I was lying here thinking of that roast chicken Robert's ma set up for us.'

'I overheard her ask Robert if you ever got fed,' Blain told him. 'She reckoned she hadn't put out enough roast potatoes, we ate that much.'

'What did Robert say to that?'

'He told her it weren't that so much as her home cooking that made us eat so much.'

'I guess that must'a pleased the old biddy,' Jephta responded. There was a pause before he continued. 'I never got a chance to tell you this afore. Blackwell has been making threats agin you and Robert and me.'

'That don't surprise me none.'

'I reckon we oughta get him afore he gets us. Some night while he's sleeping we sneak in and slit his throat.'

'Jephta, that's murder! We can't go round killing people that make threats against us!'

'What, we just wait around for him to do it to us? I heard an old soldier once spouting off about war. He reckoned the best way of defence is attack.'

'Jephta, we'll just have to be extra vigilant and keep an eye on them.'

'You reckon we oughta warn Robert?'

'It would be our duty to warn him. Maybe he can have Blackwell driven out of the gang.'

'You seemed a mite interested Sturdy's sister.' Jephta said, changing the subject.

'Huh, who me? I was just trying to be polite. Though I must admit she's very nice.'

'Nice, she's bloody gorgeous! I wouldn't mind a tumble in the hay with her.'

'Jephta, I must ask you not to be so disrespectful,' Blain said stiffly. 'Remember we're guests in this house.'

'Females are just females,' Jephta said dismissively. Blain did not answer, and Jephta continued. 'My sister was very pretty. That was when the trouble began between me and my stepfather.'

Blain was curious. Except for the time Jephta had confessed to killing his stepfather over his abuse of his mother, he had never spoken much about his family background.

'Did he hit your sister as well as hitting your ma?'

There was a pause before Jephta answered.

'Not that so much as he lusted after her.'

'Yeah, but if he was your stepfather, then he was your sister's stepfather as well. It would have been incest for him to want to . . . to do anything to her.'

'You think that stopped the old pervert?'

'Are you telling me he did?'

'Yeah.'

'Good lord!' Blain exclaimed, plainly troubled by this revelation.

'How old was she . . . your sister I mean?'

'Ten, I think.'

This was too much. Blain sat upright.

'Is that why you killed him? It was nothing to do with your ma, was it?'

'Nah, Ma was a whore. Thelma and me had different

92

fathers. I tried to look out for her, but I had to move out when Anther Hibbs moved in. He were always fighting and rowing with me. I know now that was his plan, to get me outta the way. Then he could move on Thelma. When I kicked off about it, Ma sided with him. Said as it was best for me to leave. I should'a killed him when I first met him.'

Blain lay down again, shocked by Jephta's revelations. That a father, even though he was a stepfather, could do such things was too terrible to contemplate.

'What happened to Thelma?'

'That old bastard put her on the street with the other girls. That's what she does now. Followed in Ma's footsteps. That's how I found out. I met her in a cathouse one night. She told me all about it. I knew then I would kill Hibbs.

'I stuck a knife in his guts. I watched the bastard bleed to death. Even though I was arrested for it, I never regretted killing him. I would do it all over again even if I knew I would swing.'

Blain lay there shaken by these revelations. He remembered the young girls at the house where he had met Agatha. It had never occurred to him that they were not there of their own free will. Now he began to wonder if behind every whore, there were tragic circumstances that forced them to take up the life.

Remembrance of Agatha brought a pang of guilt. Now that he had met Emelie and fallen in love with her, he wanted to come to her as chaste as he believed she was. In the darkness of the night he wrestled with his guilt. When he thought of his coupling with Agatha his face blazed with shame.

'Oh, Lord I am a sinner,' he prayed silently. 'Make me pure in body and soul. I promise I will never look at a female with lust ever again as long as I live. Make me worthy to walk in the shadow of the lovely and noble girl that has taken my heart captive.'

24

'I want you fellas along with me,' Robert told his two youthful companions. 'I have to sell that bourbon, and you might as well meet the fella we'll be dealing with. He's an old friend of mine. We went to school together. Must'a been a great school. Him and I, we both end up on the wrong side of the law.'

Alfred Mulholland was a large-bellied man, slightly older than his friend Robert. The merchant was never to be seen without a cigar stub jutting out of his mouth.

Mulholland ran a dry goods store, selling anything from mining tools to plough shares. He also owned a couple of saloons and a hotel. Sturdy and Mulholland greeted each other like old friends. There was much grinning and back-slapping. Robert introduced his companions.

'These are my guardian angels. Saved my life and then some.'

'Come in the office and tell me all about it. I ain't seen you in a while. I got some French brandy. I wasn't going to open it until the New Year, but I guess this is as good a time as any to sample it.'

The men crowded into an office at the back of the store. A desk overflowed with papers. Along the walls were shelves stacked with rifles, pistols and boxes of ammunition, along with pots and pans and household items.

'Take a seat, gentlemen, while I find some glasses.' Their host put his head outside and yelled, 'March, bring me some mugs. I got guests.'

March turned out to be a thin rake of a youngster with an

immature beard struggling to establish itself on his narrow features. He brought a handful of tin mugs, looking distractedly at his boss.

'Will this be enough, boss?'

'March, I don't know what I'd do without you. You're a pearl beyond compare. Grab a vessel, you fellas, while I get out the nectar.'

A vacant grin erupted on the youth's face before he backed out of the office.

'Poor fella is simple,' Mulholland explained. 'His mother is my cousin, so I gotta look after the unfortunate fella.'

He walked behind his desk and unlocked a cupboard.

'Voilà!' He held up a stubby glass bottle. 'French brandy!'

His guests held their tin mugs while Mulholland poured.

'To strong drink and fast women,' the merchant toasted.

Blain took a gulp and gasped as the fiery liquor burned into his throat. He was unable to stop the coughing that erupted.

'My, my, Robert, are these the fellas you led me to believe saved your miserable life? That one looks as if he should still be in school. Does his mother know he's here?'

'Don't be fooled by his youth,' Robert told Mulholland. 'This fella has fought a duel, broke outta prison and killed two lawmen that were about to blast me and my comrades to hell.'

Mulholland whistled as he stared at Blain with wide-eyed admiration.

'Well, I'll be. . . !'

'That sure is one hell-raising sonabitch,' Jephta crowed. 'When Robert brought us to his hideout a couple of fellas thought to hassle him. Blain here showed he ain't no walkover. He laid both them fellas out. It don't pay to mess with Blain Larkin.'

To Blain's embarrassment, his friends made up stories

about his exploits, and as the brandy level lowered, the tales got wilder and hairier. While his friends were doing their best to embarrass him, Blain was examining the goods on the shelves. He picked up a pistol and was weighing it in his hand when Mulholland noticed what he was holding.

'That's one of them Remingtons as is coming in now. Don't reckon much to them myself. Can't beat a good Winchester for killing. Pistol is all right in a street fight, but no good for hunting.'

Blain appraised the pistol in his hand. The butt was walnut and the barrel blued steel. He held it up and sighted along the barrel.

'Blain, seeing as you are so taken with that there pistol, I'm gonna to give it to you,' Mulholland told him, the brandy obviously working on his mood. 'A rooting-tooting hell-raiser like yourself should have a weapon worthy of his reputation. Consider this as my presentation to a dedicated desperado such as you.'

Sheepishly Blain thanked the effusive man for his gift. Mulholland insisted on handing over a box of cartridges to go with the gun, and Blain stowed the gifts about his person. Mulholland threw a benevolent arm around him.

'My good friend, Blain Larkin,' he declared, 'when you kill your next villain, have the gun inscribed: This Remington was given to me by my friend and benefactor Alfred Mulholland. Let's drink to that.'

Eventually Robert got around to the purpose of his visit. The two men hammered out a deal for the stolen bourbon.

'We got the wagon stored at the railroad depot,' Robert told him. 'We'll meet you there tomorrow morning.'

'Robert, seeing you again has stirred something in this old noggin of mine,' Mulholland said thoughtfully. 'I got wind of a gold shipment coming along. I was wondering if any of my acquaintances would be interested in making sure it fell into the right hands.'

'Gold, well that does put the pork on the fire,' Robert said. 'Tell me more. I'm all ears. I was never one for digging in the dirt for the stuff, but if it's travelling about in search of a good home then I'm willing to help myself to some of that.'

Mulholland walked to the door of his office, and pulled it closed before continuing in a lowered voice.

'There's a bank in Crow's Butte, and I'm acquainted with a clerk as works there. He passed me details about a shipment of gold. It's to come by train to the railhead and then loaded on wagons and driven to the bank. The bank is said to be impregnable. Strong construction and a new-fangled iron safe with a time lock. The trick would be to hijack the gold afore it reaches the bank.'

Robert was nodding his head in agreement.

'I guess. But it'll be heavily guarded. There would be an army of marshals assigned to protect it.'

'You have put your finger on the very thing that is the key to the operation. When you mention army, that's just what I have in mind.'

'Pour more brandy and let's hear further,' Robert told him. 'You got me all fired up with this here tale of gold bullion.'

'I have a batch of surplus army uniforms I bought up cheap,' Mulholland said. 'My idea is for you fellas, dressed up in these here uniforms, to ride up, bold as brass, all ready to escort the gold to the bank.'

'You're making me as happy as a weasel in a henhouse,' Robert enthused. 'That is one goddamn foolproof scheme if ever I heard of one.'

The pals shook hands on the deal and Mulholland agreed to bring the uniforms when he picked up the bourbon.

As a result of the intake of brandy, Blain's companions were somewhat tipsy when they left the warehouse. Blain had abstained after the first drink.

'Well fellas, what you wanna do now?' Robert asked. 'Ma expects us back home for supper. She sure took to you, Jephta, the way you gobbled up everything she set in front of you. I reckon she'll outdo herself this evening just to see if she can fill you up.'

Jephta rubbed his tummy, a pleased look on his face.

'I reckon I should settle here in Grantham? I could take care of your family while you're out hijacking bourbon and gold and the like.'

Robert roared with laughter and slapped Jephta on the back.

'Damn me, I couldn't do that. You'd bankrupt Pa within a week what with Ma buying enough vittles to keep you filled. You're a skinny little runt and yet you eat enough for a whole crew.'

'Ma said I was born hungry,' Jephta said. 'She never fed me much anyway. I guess I'm making up for all those meals I missed when I was a kid.'

'What say we go for a bath,' Robert suggested mischievously, winking at Blain.

'Hell no!' Jephta exclaimed, 'You and Blain go ahead. I'm going to sink into something much better than no damn bath.'

'And what might that be?'

Jephta smirked at Robert.

'I'm gonna find me a woman and work me up an appetite for your ma's supper tonight.'

'Yerraah!' Sturdy hollered. 'A man after my own heart. Lead on, Jephta Owens. We will go where angels fear to tread.'

Robert threw one arm around Blain and the other around Jephta, but Blain twisted out of the embrace.

'Look, I ah . . . I'm not in the mood,' Blain stammered, suddenly embarrassed, not looking at his friends.

'Blain, Blain, I guess you ain't had yourself a woman yet. I'll tell them lonesome gals to be gentle with you.'

Blain was backing away, shaking his head.

'Please, I don't want to. You and Jephta, you go ahead and enjoy yourselves. I'll go back to the house. See you there.'

Before Robert or Jephta could react Blain had turned and was walking away.

'Blain, come back!'

But Blain pretended not to hear and quickened his pace. There was only one woman in his life now. He hurried on, anxious to see Emelie again.

25

'Where is Robert?' Mrs Sturdy asked, when Blain arrived back.

'Um . . . ah . . . he was held up in town. He has some business deal he was working on.'

Blain stumbled over the lie. But before Mrs Sturdy could quiz him more, Emelie came in carrying a basket of flowers. Blain was immediately dazzled by her beauty reflected in the myriad of colours in the blooms she was carrying.

'Blain,' she beamed with obvious pleasure.

'Miss Emelie,' he stammered, becoming flustered and awkward.

'Those flowers look lovely, Emelie,' Mrs Sturdy said. 'Are you going to the cemetery now?'

'Just as soon as I get my coat, Mother.'

'Why don't you take Blain with you?'

Mrs Sturdy looked quite pleased as she suggested this. Emelie turned the full lustre of her eyes on Blain.

'I'm sure Blain wouldn't want to spend the afternoon at a cemetery.'

'Yes, I would indeed,' Blain blurted out eagerly. 'I love cemeteries.'

Mrs Sturdy wrapped a piece of apple pie and handed it to Blain.

'Just in case you get hungry.'

In a warm haze of euphoria, Blain held the door for Emelie and they left the house. His heart was beating fast as they walked together, Emelie with her flowers and Blain carrying a wedge of apple pie. The young woman set a fair pace.

'It's a longish way to the cemetery,' she informed him. 'I hope you're used to walking.'

'Oh yes, I love walking.'

Which was a lie, for Blain was first and foremost a cowboy, notorious for their reluctance to walk when they can ride.

'Whose grave is it you are to visit?' he remembered to ask.

'My brother; he died quite young. He was only three. It was before I was born. Robert said something died in mother when she lost Clemens. Then I came along and Robert reckons that saved mother from becoming morbid.'

'Gosh, it seems awful young to die.'

'Do you have any brothers or sisters?'

'Yes, I have an older brother. No, I mean, I had an older brother, but he's dead also. Something we have in common. We have both lost brothers.'

She glanced sideways at him.

'How did he die?'

Blain was silent so long Emelie did not question him further. They walked on in this manner with only occasional small talk. Blain was content to walk beside Emelie, while she was equally delighted to have him as an escort. While they walked she pointed out various landmarks to him. Eventually they came to an incline leading to the cemetery.

100

'This is Trapper's Hill,' she told him, pointing up to the cemetery. 'I come as regular as I can to tend Clemens' grave.'

Emelie stopped by a small grave with a simple wooden cross. The inscription stated that Clemens Barrett Sturdy had been gathered to the Lord at the tender age of three years. A stone vase held wilting blooms. Solemnly Emelie put her basket down and, removing the faded flowers, set them by the grave. She turned to Blain and he saw dew forming in her eyes.

'There's a trough with water over there. I'll change the water.'

'No, let me.'

Blain set down the pie he had carried from the Sturdy household and reached for the vase. In doing so their hands touched. That spark that had disconcerted Emelie the previous night ignited once more. She went rigid and stared deep into Blain's blue eyes, and a little shiver went through her body. His hand crept round the vase and imprisoned her delicate fingers. A church bell chimed out the time. One o'clock. Neither of them heard it.

'I . . . I. . .' Emelie stammered and stopped.

She tugged her hand from his, a deep blush starting up in her cheeks; the flush greatly enhancing her beauty. Blain felt a constriction in his chest and he had difficulty breathing. He took the vase from her and set it carefully beside the pie. Then he reached out and took her hands in his. She was unresisting. Her body was trembling, her mouth opening slightly as she tried to lessen the heated turmoil rising within her breast.

Gently he drew her to him. His body was on fire. He slid his hands up her arms coming to rest on her shoulders. The youngsters were very close. Blain was leaning in towards Emelie, wound up so tight he felt dizzy. She swayed nearer, unable to resist. Neither noticed the large black raven that landed on a wooden cross behind them. The sudden screech from the bird startled them both. Emelie jumped and stepped back – the magic of the moment lost.

Emelie turned and stared at the bird. It raised its wings as if to fly, but stayed where it was, balancing precariously, the wide black wings outstretched as it teetered on its perch. Her hand went to her mouth.

'The bird of death,' she whispered, the flush that had enhanced her beauty fading as the raven stared back at her with its bright button eyes.

Blain stepped forward.

'Shoo!' he hissed, angry that the bird had interrupted their moment of intimacy.

The raven continued its balancing act, its wings arched wide, looking indeed like the angel of death. Blain bent and scooped up a handful of dirt. He raised his fist to fling it, and the bird launched into flight with a frantic fluttering of wings and a long rasping caw.

The harsh sound echoed across the graveyard, and a feeling of impending doom descended on Emelie. She dropped to her knees in the dirt, bowed her head and joined her hands in prayer.

Blain stood helplessly looking down at her. When they had reached the grave Emelie had slid back her hood and now he looked with longing at the spun gold that was revealed. He wanted to reach out and touch her but something restrained him.

'Emelie,' he murmured, 'are you all right?'

She turned her dark hazel eyes upon him.

'That raven frightened me, Blain.'

He dropped to his knees beside her and once more took her hands in his.

'Emelie, I love you,' he blurted out, unable to control his emotions. 'Don't be afraid. I won't allow anything to happen to you.'

'Oh Blain, I feel this strange excitement in my breast when I look into your eyes. If that is love, then I must be in love. Let me finish with Clemens' grave. Then we can talk.'

Blain took up the vase and filled it with water from the iron trough that looked like the ones for watering horses. Emelie arranged the fresh flowers and placed the replenished vase on the grave. For a short time they bowed their heads in prayer.

Emelie removed her cloak and spread it for them to sit upon. From this vantage point they could see the rail depot. A train pulled in jetting clouds of steam. The youngsters sat very close, their arms and legs touching lightly. A pleasant glow suffused Blain. Emelie turned her head and looked into his eyes.

'How long do we have, Blain? I mean before you and Robert leave again.'

'The business your brother has with Mulholland should be finished up tomorrow morning. Then we will travel back.' He paused and a thought struck him. 'Perhaps I mightn't go back. I could stay here in Grantham.'

She reached out and took his hand. He likened it to a flower nestling in his palm, soft and delicate. Gently he raised it and touched it with his mouth. The tantalizing aroma of flowers was strong in his nostrils where she had patted and arranged the blooms for her brother's grave. He felt dizzy and excited and a strong swirl of emotions spun within.

Emelie was leaning in towards him. Gently their lips touched. A flame seared through him and he pulled her close. She gave a little mew and stretching her hands around his neck clung to him. He pushed her back and his hand sought and closed around the softness of her breast. He wriggled on top of her. For moments she was holding him, caught up in the heightened emotions of love and desire. Suddenly she struggled, her hands coming down from around his neck and pushing at this chest.

'No Blain, please . . .' she panted. 'Blain!'

His heart pounding, reluctantly he released her. She sat up, her face flushed, and patted her hair into place. Her hands smoothed at her dress, her eyes avoiding his.

'What is it, Emelie?' he asked unsteadily. 'I'm sorry if I have offended you.'

She shook her head, still not looking at him.

'Are you hungry?'

He blinked and watched her profile, aching to take her in his arms again, the desire still smouldering. She reached down for the apple pie. Prudently she edged apart from him and set the package between them, and delicately unfolded the napkin.

Staring at her while she performed this operation he could smell the cooked apple, and suddenly realized he was indeed hungry. His feelings were still in turmoil, but he forced himself to remain seated and apart from her. She broke a piece and handed it to him, still not meeting his eyes. They sat in silence nibbling the pie and looking down at the town.

'I've never been this close to a boy before,' Emelie volunteered at last. 'I . . . I feel such desires rise within me, it frightens me – sinful desires.' She blushed even as she spoke of her roused passions. 'At night my father takes us out on mission work. We go to houses where women sell themselves to men, and preach and sing hymns to them. The only reward we get for our efforts is abuse. This does not deter father. He believes he is doing God's work.'

She fell silent. Blain stared out at the town, not seeing any of it.

'It . . . it was my fault,' he said at last in a low voice. 'When I touch you, or even just look at you, I cannot help the feelings that boil up in me. I thought it was just the love I have for you, but perhaps it is sinful to desire you so. I am so sorry to have upset you.'

When she turned her head and smiled at him, he felt she had forgiven him.

'It was my fault as much as yours,' she asserted. 'But we must be vigilant. Let us treasure and respect the love we have for each other. In that way the Lord will bless us and keep us pure.'

Guilt and passion battled within Blain's breast. He wanted this lovely girl more than he had ever wanted anything. If it meant keeping his unruly passions in check, then that was what he would do. He could not risk pushing her beyond his reach by any crude behaviour on his part. Emelie stood and dusted down her clothes. Blain picked up her cloak and held it for her.

'We can take our time walking back. We have this short time together. After dinner Father wants to go preaching and Mother and I accompany him.'

And Blain was inspired to make a conciliatory gesture to make up for his behaviour earlier.

'Would your father allow me to accompany you?'

She smiled that endearing smile, put her arm through his and together they walked from the place of the dead.

'Where have those boys got to?'

Mrs Sturdy had been to the front door a dozen times, anxiously scanning the street. The supper was ready. The smell of roast meat drifted through the house, teasing Blain's nostrils.

Robert's mother had quizzed him as to her son's possible whereabouts. Feeling guilty about lying to the woman, Blain had stoutly asserted they were probably busy arranging for delivery of some goods that Robert was selling. He could hardly tell her that the last he had heard from her son was his proposal to spend time at a cathouse.

'Be at peace, woman,' her husband finally interposed. 'Your wayward son will probably turn up eventually. If we wait any longer the meal will be spoiled and we'll be late for our mission work. Serve up to us starving Christians and leave Robert's portion in the oven.'

Looking very put out, Mrs Sturdy did as her husband ordered and served up roast pork and potatoes, followed by blueberry pie and cream. Blain was ravenous and might have competed with Jephta had he been there to partake in the meal. Over the blueberry pie Blain asked Reverend Sturdy if he had any objections to his accompanying him on his evangelical work that evening.

'Blain, that is rather endearing. Robert never was interested in my mission. Now here you are offering to come with us to spread the good word. Thank you, young man. I value your support.'

The small group of missionaries gathered for the evening's proselytizing. They were mostly middle-aged females; Blain and Reverend Sturdy were the only males.

'Let us sing as we proceed on the Lord's work this night.'

The little group marched through the streets singing lustily. Blain, not knowing the words, mimed along with the singers. He was supremely happy. He was in the company of his beloved and her family. Emelie's father had praised him for helping in his missionary work. In some small measure, Blain felt he had made up for his blunder in the graveyard. There would be no more mistakes like that. His beloved was a delicate flower. He had to treat her with gentleness and compassion. He made up his own words as the company sang.

Emelie, O Love I'm by your side
I'll never leave you ever again.
Wheresoe'er your breath has given
Life to me, for I'm in heaven.

The little band of missionaries gathered on the pavement outside a large clapboard house. Lamps burned in the lower windows. There were steps leading up to the front door. Reverend Sturdy led them in hymn singing.

It was a warm night. Pedestrians looked with idle curiosity at the little group. Occasional carriages drove along the street. A hack pulled up on the far side and the passengers alighted. They were loud and merry as they crossed the road. Their obvious objective was the house where the followers of Reverend Sturdy were congregated.

'Think on my friends,' Reverend Sturdy intoned, as the men mounted the boardwalk. 'This is a house of sin, and he who enters is entering into a contract with the devil.'

There were hoots of laughter from the men.

'You're right, Reverend, there are devils in here. We come here to wrestle with them. Why don't you join us?'

'Have a thought for your souls, my friends. When the last bugle calls, how will you account for your sins?'

'The bugle can't come soon enough for us. We love a fandango as well as the next man.'

There was a roar of laughter from the revellers. They banged on the door and yelled out for admission and disappeared inside. A stern-looking woman dressed in black glared out at the gospellers before slamming the front door.

'How Satan does tempt and entrap us with his wily ways,' Reverend Sturdy intoned. 'Let us sing out loud so that those inside might hear the words and repent their sinful ways.'

They group launched into song once more. Again Blain mimed along, using his own words, expressing his love for Emelie and his yearning to spend the rest of his life with her. Suddenly the door opened and the woman in black stepped out on to the veranda.

'Stop that bawling outside my house! It's hard enough for a woman to make a living without you do-gooders driving away my customers. Now clear off afore I call the marshal.'

It was an idle threat, for no law officer would dare become entangled with a group of proselytizing Christian women.

'Ma'am, we are here not to distress you, but to set you on the path of righteousness. Repent ye of your sinful ways and follow the path of the Lord. Whosoever drinketh of the water I shall give him shall never thirst again. If you drink from the well of his mercy and goodness you will thirst no more.'

More and more females were crowding into the doorway behind the formidable figure of the madam. Some were wearing corsets and very little else, showing off bare shoulders and more leg than was acceptable to the prim parishioners of the Reverend Sturdy.

'Shame, shame!' the cry went up from the little gathering on the pavement. 'Where is your modesty?'

'And the Lord said, there is more rejoicing in the Kingdom of Heaven at one sinner returning to the bosom of the Lord.'

'Come to my bosom, Reverend,' a buxom young woman cried out as she cupped her breasts in her hands.

This induced gales of laughter. The Reverend and his little band were providing some diversion for the jaded doves. They called out insults and invitations with much hilarity. Then suddenly one of the females pushed past the madam. She was dressed in a flimsy gown that left nothing to the imagination.

'Blain,' she called, 'Oh, Blain!'

Blain stood rooted to the spot as Agatha McConnaughy

tumbled down the few steps to the boardwalk. The forward movement fluttered the gown from her legs exposing most of her lower body. Almost naked she flung herself at the mortified youth.

'Blain, oh my beloved. I thought you were dead.'

She wrapped her arms around Blain and pressed against him, murmuring endearments.

'Agatha. . . .' Blain managed to stammer.

She left off kissing his hot and sweating face, and tugged him towards the house.

'Oh, come inside, Blain. We can spend the night together. It'll be like old times. Oh Blain, my lovely boy, I'm so glad to see you.'

27

Blain tried to resist as Agatha dragged him towards the house. As the nearly naked woman manhandled him, the youngster broke into a sweat, acutely conscious that Emelie and her family were witness to his humiliation.

'Agatha . . . I . . .' he tried to protest.

She responded by pulling his head down and planting a moist kiss on his lips. He dug his heels in and dragged the eager woman to a halt.

'Agatha, I . . . It's not what you think.' Confused and embarrassed, he strove to find a way out of this dreadful situation. 'I'm engaged to be married,' he suddenly blurted.

'Blain, don't be silly. Come inside and let me show you what you have been missing.'

Agatha was irrepressible. Blain was a reminder of a happy past when she was madam of her own brothel. On the night he had been introduced to her she had fallen for his youthful innocence. He was a token of all she had never had and never would have. She had sought to recapture her adolescence that had ended before it had really started. Now he was restored to her, and her happiness was unbounded.

In desperation Blain wrenched himself free. He turned to face the Reverend Sturdy and his little flock. In vain he sought for Emelie. She was nowhere to be seen. With stricken eyes he stared at Reverend Sturdy. But before he could speak the preacher held up his hand, his face dark and angry.

'Blain Larkin, thou art a wolf in sheep's clothing. Thou art a lecher crept into the bosom of my family.'

'Reverend . . .'

Blain got no further. It was Mrs Sturdy's turn to berate him.

'I do not know what you have done to my daughter. When Emelie saw your gross behaviour she broke down in tears. As I went to comfort her she turned from me and ran from whatever sorrow you have brought upon her.' Mrs Sturdy pointed an accusing finger at him. 'Be gone, Satan!'

'Mrs Sturdy, let me explain.'

'Sinner and fornicator!' Reverend Sturdy thundered. 'Never come near my home again. There is no room for serpents amongst us. You have deceived us all.

'Come, brethren. This night has been a bitter disappointment for my family and me. We will go home now. I will find my daughter and comfort her in the hour of her need.'

There was agony in Blain's heart as he watched the little group turn and march along the street. There was no hymn singing to send them on their way. Reverend Sturdy and his wife strode at the head of the procession, leaving behind a broken Blain.

'Blain.' Agatha was tugging at his sleeve. 'Good riddance to that crowd of hypocrites.'

Her voice was low keyas she sensed the extent of Blain's distress. When he turned to her she was dismayed to see tears in his eyes. His mouth worked as he tried to say something. Abruptly he turned and stumbled down the street in the opposite direction to that of the departing religious group.

'Blain!' she called, her own face showing distress.

'Agatha, come inside,' the madam called. 'Well done! You did a good job ridding the street of that sanctimonious crowd.'

Agatha put her hand to her mouth as she turned and walked back inside. The madam was looking at her curiously, seeing the distress on her face.

'You really cared for that boy?'

Agatha burst into tears. The older woman put her arm around her and escorted her inside.

'There, there, dear, you can take the night off.'

She closed the door and turned to see two men anxiously peering at the tearful Agatha.

'What are you two boogers gawking at?'

'Pardon me, ma'am,' Robert Sturdy said. 'That youngster was a friend of ours. I wonder if we can have a word with the lady.'

Robert and Jephta accompanied Agatha to her room. The madam had insisted Robert purchase a bottle of bourbon at an inflated price to take upstairs with them. Jephta seated himself on the carpet, his back against the wall holding a glass of liquor. Robert reversed a chair and sat on that, his arms resting on the back. Agatha reclined on the bed. She had donned a bathrobe to cover her nakedness.

'We were on our way out when we heard the commotion,' Robert explained. 'When I looked outside and saw who it was, there was nothing I could do for I know the man who was leading the meeting.' Robert looked suitably embarrassed. 'In

fact it was my father. If he had found me in here I would have
been banished from the family home for ever. He is not a for-
giving man. Also, I believe it would have broken my mother's
heart.'

He fell silent. Not bothering with a glass, Agatha took a
long draught from the bottle.

'He was ashamed of me, wasn't he,' she said tearfully. 'Oh,
I'm just a silly woman.' She took another swallow. 'He said he
was to be married. I wouldn't mind that. I would have shared
him. Who is he marrying anyway? Do you know?'

'He must have meant my sister. I could see he was smitten
with her when he met her last night.'

'Last night!' Agatha wailed. 'Is . . . is she very pretty?'

'So, so. But they could not have pledged to be married so
quickly. My parents are strict about these things. It would
involve a long courtship.'

At this Agatha burst into tears again. The two men looked
on helplessly.

'If he even had come inside and talked to me,' she sobbed.
'He was such a sweet boy.'

'How . . . where did you meet him?'

Agatha sat up straighter in the bed and wiped at her eyes.

'We met in Callender. At that time I owned my own house.
He and his brother Moylan came visiting. I took to Blain
straightaway.'

The tears flowed again and she fought to contain them.

'This Moylan – was he the one as was killed in the duel?'

Sniffling into her sleeve, Agatha nodded. Recovering
somewhat she related the circumstances that had brought
both her and Blain to grief.

'I thought I would be safe from Lecroy in Crow's Butte,'
she concluded. 'Then one night Verne found me there. He
. . . he flogged me and shot my houseman, Tomas. I managed
to escape and ended up here. I lost everything. Now I work

here for Wilma Ruck.'

'This Lecroy, he sounds a right villainous piece of work.'

'A hound from hell,' Agatha agreed. 'He and his father are vile creatures. There are times I wish I were a man and I would . . . ah, what's the point of wishing.'

'We'd better get on home now. Jephta and me we been drinking most of the day. Seeing my father outside this place sobered me up some. Poor Blain, he was staying at our home. I doubt if he'll be able to go back there.'

'When you see him, tell him I still love him.' Agatha was getting emotional again. 'If he wants somewhere to stay the night I'll make him welcome.'

They left Agatha nursing the bourbon bottle. Outside on the street they turned their steps towards Robert's home.

'Hell, that Blain's a dark horse,' Jephta offered. 'Who'd'a thought he'd a lover all along? Looking at him you'd think butter wouldn't melt in his mouth.'

'Tell you the truth, it's like a Shakespearian tragedy. I don't know who to pity, Blain, Emelie, or that poor woman back in the cathouse.'

'I only hope Blain is all right. I wonder where he's at now.'

Hands jammed hard inside his pockets, Blain at that moment was wandering blindly through the town. The streets teemed with pedestrians and the roads with carriages and horsemen. In time his footsteps took him to the cemetery. He remembered Emelie's fright when the raven appeared in the graveyard.

'Emelie,' he whispered and a lump rose in his throat.

He imagined her smile and the tinkle of her laughter. Drawn by the poignant memories of that happy afternoon, Blain wandered through the graveyard seeking the place where they had sat together and pledged their love. He lay down and in time drifted off to sleep. The night crept on while he slept. Eventually daylight filtered down from a misty sky.

The coming of morning brought Blain awake. Slowly he opened his eyes. His lids chafed his eyeballs as if grains of sand were lodged there. For long moments he stared out into space.

Down below, the town was stirring into life. Smoke from cooking fires tainted the morning. Robert and Jephta had gone seeking female companionship. Blain had not gone with them. Instead he had walked unknowingly into misery.

Slowly he made his way through the graveyard. A strange calm descended upon him. His mind was made up. He resolved he would throw himself beneath the wheels of a train and end his misery.

28

Robert knocked on the bedroom door. He put his ear against the panel but there was no response.

'Emelie, can I come in?'

Still there was no reply and he waited patiently, leaning his forehead against the door.

'Emelie, it's Robert, we'll be leaving soon and I wanted to say goodbye.'

He heard her fumbling with the catch and the door opened. Emelie stood inside fully dressed. Her face was pale, her eyes, usually so bright and lively, were red-rimmed and dull. Robert stepped inside and wrapped his arms around her.

'Emelie, my beautiful sister.'

She clung to him.

'What is it Emelie? What has made you so sad?'

Still she did not speak.

'Is it something to do with what happened last night? Pa told me Blain got into a row with some female. They said you were upset. Were you fond of him?'

'Oh Robert, he knew that woman, that awful woman!'

She pulled away and walked to the window. Robert followed, reached out and stroked the back of her head. She turned a woeful face to him.

'He said he loved me. All the while he was deceiving me.'

'Emelie, I'm sure it wasn't like that. I know Blain, and from what I have observed he's an honourable fella.'

Robert knew he had to tread carefully, fearful of disclosing what he had learned of Blain's history from Agatha.

'No, Robert, you weren't there to see how it was. That woman threw herself at Blain like they were lovers. It was shameless.'

Emelie looked at her brother with stricken eyes.

'Perhaps he befriended the woman sometime in the past,' Robert said. 'He told me something of what happened before I met him. It's all mixed up with his brother that was shot. Maybe this woman was in love with this brother and when Blain went to defend him that's what got him in trouble. Things happen in the past you have no control over.

'That time when Blain rescued me I was sure I was going to die. I couldn't have changed anything. So too with Blain, he was flung into a set of circumstances he probably had no control over.'

Robert fell silent wondering if he had said enough to console his sister.

'Where is he now?' Emelie finally asked.

'I don't know. Pa said he forbade him from returning here. I really don't know where he is. Unfortunately I can't stay to look for him. We have to get to the rail depot to complete my business deal. I just wanted to say goodbye afore we go. Could I take a message to Blain if I see him again?'

'There is nothing I have to say to him. Just you take care and come back safe.'

Brother and sister embraced.

'Find it in your mind to forgive Blain,' Robert whispered. 'Do not let this hurt fester in your heart.'

A while later he departed along with Jephta for the railroad depot where they had stored their wagon with the bourbon.

The railhead was in turmoil. Passengers carrying bags peered into carriages; others were leaving the depot, looking for passage in the horse-drawn carriages. Some were trudging under their own steam into town. Everyone seemed seized with urgency.

Oblivious of the noise and bustle, Blain headed for the far end of the platform. Massive metal monsters puffed clouds of steam into the morning air. Couplings clanked their metallic refrain. Men shouted greetings and farewells. Railroad officials hollered at passengers telling them of train arrivals and departures. Blain reached the edge of the platform and stopped – waiting for the train that would take him to the other side of death.

I will think only of Emelie, he reflected as he looked down at the steel rails, and wondered if she would ever think of him as she made her way in life. She would meet some other man, a man worthy of her love.

'I wish you happiness, Emelie,' he murmured.

It would be best if she forgot him. All the things that had happened to him in some way tainted the people around him, the encounter with Agatha, the death of Moylan, the trial and sentence of hanging. The only good and beautiful event in his life had been meeting Emelie.

A steam whistle shrieked wildly – the demented cry of a mischievous sprite. The sound reminded Blain of yesterday and the raven in the graveyard – the bird of ill-omen. The heavy goods train was moving up the line. Blain jumped.

His head hit the steel rail and he saw stars. He thought he heard someone call his name, but by then he was turning his face towards the train coming down the track. Brakes squealed as the driver saw him fall on to the rails. Blain lay dazed and apathetic, watching the train rush towards him.

'Blain!'

Hands seized him and pulled at his jacket. He was enveloped in a cloud of steam and the screaming of tortured metal, as brakes were jammed tight in a futile effort to stop in time. A man was sitting on the cinders beside the tracks holding him in his arms.

'Larkin, dear God, Larkin. Are you all right?'

Blain opened his eyes and gazed dully at the concerned face of Alfred Mulholland.

'Wha . . . What. . . !' he croaked.

Beside them the wheels were slowing and the train was drawing to a halt. Mulholland stood and pulled him to his feet. The train finally ground to a stop. An anxious driver was leaning out of his cab staring back at Blain and Mulholland. He threw his hands out in a gesture of enquiry. Mulholland waved back to indicate everything was under control.

'Come on, can you walk?'

Blain nodded and felt a trickle of blood on his temple where he had hit the rail. He was dazed and confused and not quite in full control. Mulholland guided him towards the front of the train.

'He OK?' the driver called as they neared the engine, his face red and sweaty beneath his peaked cap.

'Sure,' Mulholland called. 'Just shook up a bit.'

They passed around the front of the engine and climbed

up on the platform.

'I spotted you standing there, and was coming across to speak when I saw you fall. What happened, did you have a dizzy spell?'

Blain nodded and his head hurt, and he felt lightheaded and staggered slightly.

'Whoa there, young fella, let's get you sitting down.'

Mulholland settled Blain on a bench. While Blain slumped dejectedly, his head in his hands, his rescuer pulled a flask from an inside pocket.

'Here, take a swig of this. I'll take a look at that gash on your head.'

'Mulholland, are you trying to get that fella drunk?' a voice bellowed.

Mulholland jumped and looked around, and relaxed when he recognized the speaker.

'Robert, can't you look after your fellas? I had to rescue the youngster off the goddamn tracks. Gave me a fright, falling in front of a train like that.'

'Blain, what the hell have you been up to?'

Blain looked sheepishly at Robert.

'Sorry, I fell over. Howdy Jephta.'

As they talked, a train drew level with much huffing and puffing and clanking of wheels so that further conversation was difficult.

'Your stuff's all ready,' Robert yelled in Mulholland's ear. 'Bring your wagon across.'

Blain felt drained and deeply depressed as he watched the whiskey being unloaded. When he made an attempt to help he was told to take things easy. Mulholland pulled out a kerchief and told Blain to hold it against his forehead to stem the blood leaking from the gash on his head. The youngster sat, detached and empty as his friends worked.

Robert and Jephta transferred the barrels of bourbon to

Mulholland's wagon, and in turn took on board a few bales of army uniforms roped together. The storekeeper had also brought much needed supplies to take back with them. When the transfer was complete, Mulholland shook hands all around, and wishing them success in their new venture, drove off. Once the storekeeper had departed, Sturdy turned to Blain and Jephta.

'Climb on board the wagon, you two. Time for us to mosey on back to home sweet home.'

Mulholland was driving the wagon loaded with the stolen bourbon when he noticed a young woman hurrying along the boardwalk. She was pale of face and her hair was being tossed about as she hurried along. It was obvious she was in some distress. Mulholland drew up alongside her.

'Miss Sturdy, I do declare! Have you come to see Robert off? I'm afraid you're too late.'

'I . . . I . . .' she stuttered breathlessly. 'Was he alone?'

'Why no, he had his two buddies with him, the ones he calls his guardian angels.'

'Jephta and Blain – were they all right?'

'Jephta was, but poor Larkin, he fell in front of a train.'

Before he could continue Emelie's eyes opened wide, her face paled even more and she swayed unsteadily. Hastily Mulholland climbed from the wagon.

'Miss Sturdy, you don't look at all well. Sit up here.'

Mulholland helped her up on to the seat.

'I have a little brandy,' he said, and took the flask from his pocket, the same one he had offered Blain.

'What have you done with him?' Emelie asked, her eyes dark pools of anguish.

'Done with whom, miss?'

Mulholland was busy undoing the flask and pouring a measure into the cap.

'Blain. . . .'

'Oh, I handed him over to your Robert. Here, take a sip of this.'

So distracted was Emelie she took the brandy and tipped it back. Unused to anything stronger than milk or coffee, the liquor made her gag and brought on a coughing fit. Mulholland looked on helplessly.

'Are they . . . where will they bury him?' she managed to gasp eventually.

'Bury? Bury who, miss?'

'Blain,' she whispered.

'Bury him, dear me no, miss! He ain't dead, just a bit shook up. I managed to pull him clear.'

The brandy was having an effect, and colour was returning to Emelie's cheeks.

'I never got to say goodbye,' she sniffled, feeling light-headed and woeful.

To Mulholland's consternation she burst into tears. He watched helplessly and had a sudden insight.

'Blain Larkin,' he murmured under his breath, 'you lucky young devil!'

29

On the trip back Blain rode in the front seat with Robert while Jephta rode inside. No reference was made regarding the events in Grantham. Robert kept his counsel, and Blain certainly did not wish to go over the unhappy experience that had driven him to throw himself in front of a train. They drove in silence for some time before Blain felt constrained to make smalltalk.

Robert was relieved to see Blain's moody silence easing. Since finding Blain at the station with Mulholland he wondered if the youth had fallen in front of the train or jumped. He still didn't know the answer. He was also wary of opening up on the subject of Blain's relationship with Emelie.

As well as the complication of Emelie being his sister, Robert was also privy to Blain's history and of his involvement with Agatha McConnaughy. It was a tricky situation, and until Blain broached the subject Robert could only wait. In an effort to lighten the awkward atmosphere the outlaw leader burst into song.

My love was a sodbuster's son
When first my tender heart he won,
I gave my heart into his care
E'en tho' my mother said beware.
My father was a proud rich man
My love from me he did ban.
He was head of the recruitment board
My lover's name he did put forward.
I remember the day he said farewell
And told me that what ere befell
He would return and we would marry
So I kissed him and told him not to tarry.

The ballad went on to tell the tragic tale of the soldier's death at Gettysburg and the subsequent despair of his young lover. In spite of his bleakness of spirit, Blain wondered if it was the worst singing he had ever heard, but kept his observations to himself. Finishing his ditty Robert grinned at him.

'I know what you're thinking, Blain. You don't have to say it. When I was a little boy Pa used to take Sis and me on missionary work. He always instructed me to hum along and not concern myself with singing. He reckoned when I was born, the Angel of Music must have been having a day off.'

The awkwardness eased, and for the next hour or so Robert regaled his companions with tales of his childhood and growing up in a strict religious household. The occasional mention of Emelie caused Blain's heart to constrict but he did his best to hide his agitation.

'I guess my pa despaired of me from an early age,' Robert remarked after a story involving the theft of apples from a neighbour's orchard. 'I still remember the paddling I got for that. I limped for a week after. I reckon that's when I started to go wrong. Uh! Uh!'

The last remark was prompted by the sudden appearance of two horsemen. They hauled their horses on the trail ahead, effectively blocking the wagon's progress.

'Howdy, fellas,' Robert called. And in an aside to his companions. 'Looks like this might be trouble.'

Blain put his hand on the handle of the Remington revolver that had been returned to him by Robert.

'Hold up there.'

The man who spoke was heavily bearded with blunt features. In his hand he gripped a large pistol held casually in front of his belly. Mounted behind him was a youngster, hatless, with close-cropped hair and a sour look. Robert called out to the team and hauled on the reins.

On the other side of the trail two more men appeared. One was of slim build and had an unkempt beard straggling down on to his upper chest. His companion had greying face hair thick around his mouth and chin. Without exception they all exuded menace, not least because they were holding guns. Blain likened them to wolves eyeing up prey, and felt a shiver of apprehension.

'Well, well, well, Douglas Barger,' Robert said. 'What brings you across here? Last I heard you was in prison.'

'Ain't no prison built that can hold me. What you toting in that there wagon?'

'Ain't nothing of any worth. Just some old army uniforms I was hoping to sell on the reservation. I'm buddy with a Shoshone scout. He tells me his people will pay well for uniforms. Makes them feel they got potent magic when they wear 'em.'

'You always was a goddamn good liar, Sturdy. Musta got it from your preacher pa. How's that pretty sister of yourn? She musta grown some since I last seed her.'

'Leave my family outa this, Barger,' Sturdy said tightly. 'You sully their name just by speaking about 'em.'

'Hah, touch on a delicate subject, eh Sturdy? Your pa so holy I bet he don't even undress in front of your ma. Probably does it with his clothes on. Are you even sure you an' your sis are his? I allus said you was a bastard in more ways than one.'

This observation was followed by a bellow of raucous laughter.

'Hell, Doug, let's quit the jawing and take the goddamn wagon and be on our way.'

The man who spoke was the straggly bearded one on the opposite side of the trail.

'Sorry about this, Sturdy. We need that wagon for a little job we're planning. We propose to rob a stagecoach. An' what better way to stop it than with a broken-down wagon blocking the trail.'

'You always was a dumb son of a bitch, Barger,' Robert told him heatedly. 'This wagon ain't broken. The only thing that's broken is your goddamn brain.'

Barger laughed again.

'Stop stalling, Sturdy. I don't wanna shoot you, but if you don't do as I say and give over that goddamn wagon, there will be shooting. An' seeing as you're outnumbered two to one, it seems to me you'rn at a big disadvantage.'

'Huh! Often a man's mouth has broken his nose. I don't see nothing as I wouldn't kick outa my way without a second thought.'

Robert paused and pretended to look around.

'This is a lonely place to die, Barger. You sure you don't wanna back up and live to see another day?'

'Hells bells, Barger, let's have done with this chin-wagging.' The bearded man raised his pistol. 'Just shoot the boogers and be done with it.'

Blain was almost deafened as a rifle blasted out from the wagon behind him. The man who had just spoken jerked in the saddle and a red star appeared in his chest. Robert shoved Blain so he tumbled out of the wagon. And then all hell broke loose.

Robert was standing up in the wagon, his gun out and firing at the hold-up men. They were firing back, but hindered because the sudden blast of gunfire had startled the horses and they were plunging about.

Blain sat up and fumbled for his Remington. A bullet ricocheted off a wheel hub and burned across his shoulder. He almost dropped his gun, but managed to retain his grip and point it at the horsemen. Two were sprawled in the dirt. Aiming his gun, he fired. A horse squealed and staggered across the trail shaking its head. The man astride it slid to the dirt and Blain fired at him. Above him in the wagon Robert's pistol clicked on empty. He could hear Jephta cursing and shooting from inside the wagon.

With a great shout Barger urged his horse forwards, the hand with his pistol held out straight in front of him.

Clutching his gun two-handed, Blain pointed and fired at the huge shape bearing down on him. The horse suddenly plunged to its knees, throwing the rider. Barger catapulted forwards, hurtling straight towards Blain. In a panic the youngster kept pulling the trigger, but the bullets did not stop the big man who had been thrown from his horse.

Like a fall of rock, Barger crashed into Blain and the revolver was knocked from his hand. Brutal hands gripped the youngster's throat. Blain struggled futilely, but was helpless beneath the crushing weight. Guttural snarling sounds were coming from the big man as he throttled the youngster.

Blain clawed at the callused hands clamped around his neck. It was like trying to part a tightly knotted rope. Blain's mouth was wide open as he strained against both the dead weight on top of him and the hands squeezing his throat. As he struggled, black spots floated across his vision and he was slowly losing consciousness.

'Die, you son of a bitch,' Barger mouthed, and spittle dribbled on to Blain.

It was then Blain realized the thing he had wanted back in Grantham was being granted him. His death was coming at the hands of a brutal bandit. He stopped struggling as he felt his life slipping away. A vision of a young female floated across his fading senses. Perversely it was not the woman he had given his heart to, but the woman he had met back in Callender: Agatha McConnaughy opened her arms to him, and together they sank into darkness.

30

'Blain. Goddamn it man, open your goddamn eyes!'

Robert was bent over the youngster, alternatively slapping his cheeks and shaking him. Jephta hovered nearby anxiously watching.

'Where's he hit?'

'Hell I can see. There's so much blood.'

And indeed the unconscious youth was covered in gore.

'Come on Blain, snap outta it. Don't you die on me!'

Sprawled nearby lay the body of Barger with most of his head missing. Jephta had leapt from the wagon to see his friend being throttled by the burly gang leader. He had rammed the muzzle of his rifle in Barger's ear and pulled the trigger. The heavy slug had broken open the outlaw's head, rather as might happen to an overripe melon when dropped on a hard surface. The resulting wash of blood and brain had splashed over Blain.

'Bring some water,' Robert ordered.

When Jephta handed him the flask, Robert poured it over Blain's face. The youngster twitched and coughed. He opened his eyes and looked up at Robert who was shaking his head as he gazed down at him.

'You got some kinda death wish, Blain,' Robert exclaimed. 'First you fall under a damned train, and now you fall under that son of a bitch Barger. Where are you hurt?'

'Huh!'

Blinking and grimacing Blain pushed himself upright. He looked down and saw the blood.

'I've been shot.'

Robert was probing around Blain's chest and stomach.

'Where does it hurt?'

'Everywhere,' Blain replied, his voice hoarse.

He put his hand up and massaged his throat.

'He was strangling me.'

'I can't find no wound. Dammit, I have a feeling that's Barger's blood.'

'Fella's gotta lotta goddamn blood,' Jephta remarked. 'Bled like the fat pig he is.'

Robert helped Blain to stand. The youngster leaned against the wagon.

'Jephta, check on those other fellas,' Robert said. 'See if any survived.' He turned back to Blain. 'You hav'ta thank Jephta for saving you. It was him as blew Barger's head apart. Saved your bacon.'

There came a shot, and Robert swung around, his hand on his gun.

'Jephta?' he called.

'It's all right. One of them weren't dead, but he is now.'

'Goddamn it, Jephta, you got the morals of a loco coyote.'

'The no good son of a bitch tried to kill us. I reckon in this world, it's kill or be killed.'

'Look, just because we're outside the law don't mean we gotta act like savages.' Robert was gazing at Jephta and frowning. 'What if it had been you lying there with a slug in you and someone came up and shot you in the head? We have to try and bring a little compassion into the world. It's what separates us from the animals in the jungle.'

'Hell, that's what I was doing,' Jephta retorted. 'The fella was in pain so I put an end to his suffering. If a buffalo was lying wounded and a wolf came along it would do the same.'

Robert pursed his lips and made as if to reply, but ended up shaking his head.

'OK, let's get back on the road.'

The remainder of the journey to the outlaw town was without incident. They pulled up outside the hotel. Some of the gang members came out to greet them.

'Howdy, Sturdy. How'd the trip go?'

'Good! We sold the bourbon and bought in supplies. Help us unload, and then we can take the horses down the livery.'

More men arrived on the scene.

'We'll have a well-earned drink and then I'll tell you boys some good news about a gold bullion job.'

The mention of gold bullion brought a surge of excitement amongst the outlaws.

'Gold, that brings a warm glow to this old heart.'

'Heart! Huh, you ain't gotta heart, Bob Parsledge. There's a lump of lava lodged in that old chest of yourn.'

'At least I gotta heart, Midge. You ain't got any room in that skinny frame of yourn for anything, only a stomach and a bladder.'

The outlaws unloaded the supplies, mostly coffee and hard tack and flour and beans along with jerky. Toby Grattan was hauling out the bundle of uniforms when Robert stopped him.

'Leave them there for now, Toby. We'll have a meeting, and I'll tell you how that bundle of duds is gonna earn us a fortune in gold.'

Inside the hotel the gang crowded around Robert, eager to hear his plans. The mention of gold had excited them. When everyone had drinks served up, Robert outlined the plan Mulholland had concocted.

'So when the train carrying the gold arrives in Crow's Butte, we ride up in our uniforms and undertake to escort the bullion so that no nasty bandits can steal it.'

There was a roar of laughter from his listeners and excited chattering broke out.

'Goddamn, that's the slickest deal I ever did hear of.'

'You mean, they'll hand the gold over to us, just like that?'

'Howdy marshal, the president of the United States has asked me to deliver this gold safe and sound into my own personal bank.'

There was one dissenting member.

'I never heard of such a goddamn fool plan,' Blackwell interjected. 'You think them officials are dumb? You'll need papers and passes and all sorts of stuff to pull it off. I should know. I was a sergeant for five years. Nothing moves in the army excepting you got a piece of paper authorizing it.'

This observation brought the mirth to an end.

'My informant thought of all that,' Robert told him. 'He got hold of passes and official documents from his contact in the army – the same one as got him the uniforms. We wave them around and everyone will be convinced we're bona fide army.'

'You're a damn fool to think you can pull this off,' Blackwell said sourly. 'Get us all killed, most likely.'

'Trust me, Blackwell. We'll all be rich. Worry about how you gonna spend your share of the gold. So get yourself a uniform, and seeing as you are ex-army you can instruct these new recruits how to act when they're in uniform.'

There was more discussion, and in spite of Blackwell's reservations, the men were optimistic as to the outcome of their venture. Eventually Robert called a halt to the talk.

'Get them uniforms distributed,' he told Blain. 'We have today and tomorrow to get used to being in the army. Jump to it. We'll want to make a good impression.'

Obediently Blain went outside and climbed into the back of the wagon.

'All men to assemble for issue of uniforms,' he bawled.

The first to arrive was Wilbur Borgman. He grinned up at Blain.

'Larkin, good to see you again. What you got?'

'Uniforms for our brave boys.'

Standing on the tailgate Blain unpacked the garments, bringing forth an outburst of hoots and cheers.

'Hell's bells, goddamn genuine army uniforms!'

The distribution went well. Blain dished out tunics and caps. He was so engrossed in his task he took no notice of the men coming forward to claim a uniform. He would hand out the clothing to a pair of hands, then grab up the next batch.

'Goddamn uppity bastard – if you think you can come here and lord it over us, you got another think coming.'

Blain looked up in surprise. So far the banter had been good-natured amongst the men, but this was something different. There at the tailgate stood Blackwell and his partner Willer.

'The first chance I get you will die,' Blackwell growled. 'You ain't coming out of this raid alive. You've caused me enough grief. I aim to get even, and the only way I'll be satisfied is when you and that other son of a bitch, Owens, are daid.'

For a moment Blain did not know how to respond. The events of the last two days had left him traumatized. He had been mechanically carrying out his tasks, trying not to think of the dead spot in his soul left there when Emelie walked out of his life. Now the hate-filled face of Blackwell glared up at him, and the knot that he had kept tight inside abruptly unravelled. He lashed out with his boot and hit Blackwell square on the bridge of the nose. With a startled yelp Blackwell fell back, tripped over his feet and went down. Willer took one look at Blain's enraged face and backed away.

'You bastard, you're dead!' he yelled, as he fumbled for his pistol.

At that point Robert emerged in the street. Seeing Blackwell sprawling in the dirt and Blain looking as if he was ready to launch himself on top of Willer, Sturdy drew and fired almost as one action. The shot stopped Willer. He looked around startled and not a little frightened.

'Willer,' Robert bellowed, 'what the hell's going on?'

'Sonabitch booted Blackwell. He's a mad dog as needs putting down.'

'Goddamn it, can't you two leave Larkin alone? We're about to pull off the robbery of the century, and you get to fighting.' Robert turned his attention to Blain. 'What the hell you playing at, Larkin? All you gotta do is hand out goddamn uniforms and you can't do that without getting into a fight.'

Blain blinked; the red haze of madness fading.

'Blackwell tripped and fell against the tailgate. Bust his nose I imagine.'

'Goddamn liar,' Willer yelled. 'I saw him kick Blackwell. I saw it with my own goddamn eyes.'

Robert looked at Blackwell holding a hand to a bloody nose. He looked back up at Blain. There was nothing in the youth's face to tell if he was lying or not.

'Blackwell, try and be more careful. Collect your uniform.'

Holding his hand to his bleeding nose Blackwell opened his mouth to protest.

'Now, Blackwell,' Sturdy yelled. 'Maybe you don't want in on the raid.'

Muttering cusses and threats, the malcontents took the proffered clothing. Watching them walk away, Blain knew that sometime in the future there would have to be a reckoning. He went back to his job of handing out uniforms. He was humming as he worked, seemingly unaware that it was the hymn he had sung on the last occasion he had been with Emelie Sturdy and the little band of missionaries.

31

The bank in Crow's Butte was a single-storey brick building. Clustered around were other business premises – hotels, saloons, stores, a livery and blacksmith, stage line, a telegraph office and a barber's shop. Heavy wooden doors that were open during the day protected the property at night. As additional security the windows were faced with iron grilles. There was an armed security guard who made regular patrols.

Verne Lecroy had an office in the bank where he was supposed to oversee financial business. However, Lecroy was more interested in entertaining cronies and certain lady friends. In order to pander to his personal preferences the office contained a well stocked liquor cabinet.

The day-to-day running of the bank he left to his staff, which suited them admirably. With no one to overlook their behaviour, shady dealings were the norm. Oblivious to all this, Verne lolled around in his office and acted the big shot banker.

Lecroy was reading the Crow's Butte Chronicle when there was a knock on his office door. Quickly he stuffed the newspaper under the desk and opened a folder, picking up a pen.

'Yeah,' he called.

The door opened and a head poked inside.

'Some people to see you, Mr Lecroy. Mr Blackwell and Mr Willer.'

'Just give me a minute to finish this, and then show them in.'

Moments later the door knocked again and the clerk ushered two men inside. Verne eyed them up in surprise and some concern. The men who entered had the look of drifters. This was not the normal set he was used to dealing with. One was a big man with a burly frame, probably in his late forties with an unshaven and craggy face. His companion was leaner and meaner, if that were possible. Verne didn't offer them a seat. Instead he opened a drawer and laid his hand on the pistol he stored there.

'Howdy, gentlemen, and what can the great bank of Lecroy do for you?'

'Ain't what you can do for us, it's what we can do for you, mister,' the big one growled. 'Got some information you might wanna pay us for.'

'That so, let's hear it.'

'First off, we gotta have a promise of a reward for what we gonna tell you.'

Lecroy's hand closed on the butt of the pistol.

'Fella, you don't look like you got anything of value to tell me. I guess you to be down on your luck and trying to pull a fast one. Well, I tell you now, it's not going to work.'

The men glanced at each other.

'What d'you think, Willer? Should we let this dumbass banker walk into a raid on that gold shipment he's fixing to take charge on?'

Lecroy was suddenly alert.

'What gold shipment?' he asked, trying not to act surprised.

'You mean you don't know about that gold as is being delivered to the railhead in two days time? My, my, Mr Banker, you oughta keep up to date with what goes on in your own bank.'

'You know, Blackwell, we oughta open a bank. We could

133

run it smarter than this stuffed shirt with cow dung for brains.'

'Wait, wait,' Lecroy spluttered, trying to hang on to his temper.

His inclination was to take out his pistol and order the men to get the hell out of his sight. But the gold bullion was supposed to be a closely guarded secret. The transaction was conducted under strict security. Now these saddle bums were claiming to know all about it.

'If he don't know about the gold, then he sure as hell don't know about the heist being planned,' Willer said. 'Mebby we wasting our time. You are Lecroy? Not some jumped-up little clerk standing in for him? You don't look like a banker. You ain't fat enough.'

'How come you know about these affairs?' Lecroy asked, trying to ignore the insults. 'I ain't saying there is a gold shipment, but supposing there was anything in your speculations, how come a couple of . . .' Lecroy hesitated as he took in the disreputable appearance of the two men, unsure how to describe them, '. . . fellas like you would come to know of these things?'

The big one tapped the side of his nose with his forefinger.

'Just say we know all about your bank, and all about times and dates for delivery of a certain gold shipment coming in from . . .' Blackwell broke off and nibbled as his fingernail as if in deep thought. 'Now where did that fella tell us, Jordan? Damn me my memory is terrible. Marksville? Did he mention Marksville? Yeah, I think he said as it was coming in from Marksville. By train, mebby?'

It was too much for Lecroy. He took out the pistol and at the same time pressed a handle that sounded an alarm out front.

'This is some kinda trick. You fellas had better tell where you got this information or face the consequences.'

'Hell mister, you got no call to pull a gun on us,' Blackwell growled. 'We come here to help you.'

The door opened and an elderly clerk poked his balding head inside.

'Fetch Tex Plant,' Lecroy snapped. 'Pronto!'

The two outlaws glanced at each other.

'Plant? Hell, I know Plant,' Blackwell growled. 'He'll surely vouch for us.'

'We'll see.'

The door opened again and Plant edged inside, gun drawn.

'Boss?'

'These two hellions claim they know about a gold shipment coming up here by rail.'

'I'll be damned,' Blackwell exclaimed. 'Tom Plant.'

The gunman frowned at the men.

'Blackwell, what the hell are you doing here?'

'You know them?' Lecroy queried.

'Sure I know these galoots. We were in the army together. What's going on?'

'Can you vouch for them?'

'Well, I wouldn't leave any valuables lying around while these two are on the loose. But yeah, you wanna couple of rannies as will do some dirty work for you, they're the men to hire.' Hedger holstered his gun. 'What you fellas up to?'

'We got good information about a raid some owlhoots are planning, and figured the bank would be so grateful they would give us a reward. Instead you all go pulling guns on us.'

32

The sun beat down mercilessly. The troop had been riding for a couple of hours, sweating in their unfamiliar uniforms. Men grumbled and cursed, and Sturdy tried to mollify them by reminding them of the riches that awaited them.

'You'll live in luxury the rest of your lives,' he told them. 'Never have to steal and run from the law again. You'll have women throwing themselves at you, anxious to help you spend all that dough.'

Blain looked across at his friend Jephta, looking relaxed in contrast to Blain's own state of agitation. Since coming back from Grantham, Blain had been moody and fretful. To counteract this black depression he had kept himself busy. It also helped that he had made a conscious decision not to think of the events that had driven him to make the abortive attempt to throw himself under a train.

He realized in the next few hours he might once more have the opportunity to die. A bullet from a lawman might possibly just do the thing for him. When Robert returned home to his family, he might casually mention the young man who had disgraced himself during his visit.

'We never saw his body. He might be buried anywhere. Or lying out in the bush being picked over by coyotes and buzzards.'

'We will pray for his soul,' Reverend Sturdy would answer. 'Though I doubt he's roasting in hell now.'

Perhaps Emelie would shed a little tear for him. And on second thoughts Blain doubted she would be moved to tears over his death. When next she went to the cemetery she might put an extra bloom on the grave of her brother.

'That's for that vile creature who deceived me.'

And Agatha. What of Agatha? For the first time he wondered how she came to be in Grantham. There was no rational explanation as to why she, of all people, had stumbled across him when he was in the company of Emelie.

I am doomed, he thought. And suddenly he was convinced he would die that very day. The thought did not disturb him unduly. I will surely die today, he repeated to himself, and a strange calm settled over him.

'Jephta.'

'Yeah.'

'I guess I was in love with Emelie.'

Jephta turned his head towards him.

'Sure, I know that.'

'You know! What the hell d'you mean, you know?'

'We could all see it. You were hanging round her like a dog in heat.'

'It wasn't like that. I just loved her for herself. She was pure and gentle and good. I guess I didn't deserve her. I never told you what happened that night afore we came back.'

'You didn't need to. We saw it all.'

'What you mean?' Blain asked, frowning.

'Robert and me, we were in that damn cathouse when you and the Holy Joes started hymn singing outside.'

Blain gaped at his friend.

'You . . . you saw . . . you and Robert?'

Jephta couldn't stop grinning.

'We had to console Agatha some afterwards. She was all broke up about you. Told us you were childhood sweethearts.'

'Dammit, it wasn't like that at all. I. . . .'

He got no further for Jephta burst out laughing. Blain glared at his friend but his ire did not last.

'Jephta, when you get back to Grantham, tell Emelie I never meant no harm. All that happened long afore I met her.'

'Why don't you tell her yourself? Or better still, have a leg or an arm shot off. When she sees you crippled she'll take pity on you and forgive you everything.'

Blain was about to reply that he would not survive to return to Grantham when the sight of Robert lifting his arm interrupted his morbid predictions. The group halted and the gang boss turned to face them.

'Right fellas, remember we're soldiers. Don't slouch in the saddle. Try and keep good order.'

In reasonable formation they went forwards. Anyone watching would not doubt this was a troop of soldiers on some exercise. Ahead of them they could see a train idling in the goods yard.

Marshal Les Howarth was in charge of the deputies assigned to guard the gold bullion. A lean, swarthy man with a walrus moustache, he observed the soldiers coming towards the rail depot. He had positioned men around the yard armed with rifles. The marshal himself was standing behind a cart, conveniently placed so he had a view of the approach road, and which provided him with cover if shooting started.

The wagons ferrying the gold to the train station were expected to arrive soon. Howarth was edgy. He had been told the gold was valued at three-quarters of a million dollars. He also learned that details of the transaction had leaked out, and a troop of bogus soldiers would try and hijack the gold.

He only hoped his deputies held their fire until the outlaws were given a chance to surrender. The last thing he wanted was a bloodbath with him in the middle of it. Howarth saw the captain raise his hand, and the troop came to halt. The captain rode forward.

'Who's in charge here?'

Howarth stayed where he was, shielded by the cart. He had a wad of tobacco in his mouth and spat before speaking.

'I'm Marshal Howarth,' he said. 'What's the army doing up here?'

'Captain Sanderson, sir,' Sturdy told him. 'We've been detailed to provide an escort for the gold. Where do you want us to deploy?'

Howarth spat.

'No one told me about no army escort. You got papers, orders, anything like that?'

'Sergeant.'

Sturdy turned to Keith Edmonton, one of the older men, and held out his hand expectantly.

'Give those orders up here.'

'Yes, Sir.'

Edmonton made a good show of patting his pockets and searching his saddle bags.

'Come on, come on,' Sturdy said impatiently.

'Here, sir.'

The sergeant passed a wad of notes forward, which Sturdy then offered to the marshal.

'Now tell us how you want us deployed and we'll work with you to deliver the gold safely.'

'Captain,' Howarth said heavily and spat a stream of tobacco juice between the legs of Sturdy's horse. 'I got thirty armed deputies surrounding this place. Right now they should be aiming rifles at you and your soldiers. Do you want to surrender now, or shall I give the order to start firing? If you give up your weapons peaceable you'll face nothing worse than a spell in jail. If you resist, I can tell you now a lot of those fellas you got there dressed up as soldiers will end up daid.'

'What the hell, Marshal?' Sturdy exclaimed. 'What damn fool game are you playing at? We're on the same goddamned side.'

'Not from where I'm standing. My information is that a fella name of Robert Sturdy will come in here with a gang of outlaws, dressed as soldiers, and try to hijack a shipment of gold. Tell me if I'm wrong, and I'll apologize and hand in my badge.'

Sturdy sat dumbfounded, realizing they had been rumbled. The only thing was to retreat and hope to extricate himself and his men from this bad situation.

'Marshal, there surely has been some mistake. I have no option but to order my men to return to barracks.'

Then the thing Marshal Howarth feared happened. One of his deputies, no doubt made nervous by the standoff, fired off a shot.

'Hold your fire,' he yelled.

It was too late. A veritable blizzard of lead was unleashed upon the bogus soldiers.

33

The sudden barrage spooked the outlaws' horses and they plunged about in panic. Blain's horse skittered to one side as he wrestled with the reins. A piece of lead whistled past his head. As an ex-cowboy he was an expert rider and quickly had his mount under control.

Blain pulled his Remington and looked for a target. Some

of the attackers in their eagerness had left cover and were advancing across the yard towards the panic-stricken outlaws. He fired at a man who jerked back and fell away. More deputies were moving up, and Blain emptied his gun at them, not sure if he was hitting anything. It was a desperate attempt to slow them down, but the lead coming his way didn't appear to diminish any.

'Retreat!'

Robert was yelling at the gang. Some men were down, knocked from their horses, some were slumped in the saddle. A few were doing as Blain and firing back. One of those was Jephta, who fired steadily at the lawmen.

'Get away!'

Robert was waving frantically at the gang. Those who could wheeled their mounts and forged away. Blain pouched his empty weapon and took off. The depleted band surged back up the road, down which only minutes before they had ridden with so much hope. They had no sense of direction – just running from the ambush, every man for himself. Back in the railhead Marshal Howarth was urging his deputies to get their horses.

'Mount up!' he yelled. 'We'll have those sons of bitches afore they get away.'

A couple of riders were coming up to the yard and called out to him.

'Marshal, don't let them get away. I want every one of them goddamn jackaroos caught and hanged.'

'We sure will, Mr Lecroy.'

'How the hell you let them escape?'

'Some damn fool let off his gun too soon. I was hoping to get them to surrender. Anyway, they ain't going nowhere. I got men posted on the road a mite back. Once they hear the shooting they'll wait in ambush. I got some good men up there. We'll have them sandwiched 'atween us.'

141

A rider came up leading a horse.

'Here's your mount, Marshal. Everybody's ready.'

Once he was mounted the marshal waved his arm in the air.

'Let's go get those varmints. I want none of them to escape.'

Ahead of the posse the remnants of the outlaw band were flogging their horses in a mindless flight. They had come to a stretch of trees when they saw a couple of wagons pulled across the road.

'They've got us cut off,' Robert yelled. 'Get in them trees. It's every man for himself. We'll meet up back at the hideout.'

A few shots were fired from the barricade, but the distance was too great for accurate shooting. The gang wheeled their horses and plunged into the trees. In moments the road was empty, leaving the lawmen unsure what to do next. They heard the thunder of hoofs and the posse from Crow's Butte came surging up the road.

'Hell's bells,' Marshal Howarth roared as he pulled up at the barricade. 'You must'a seen them. They must'a come this way.'

'In the woods,' a thickset man called. 'They lit out into those there trees.'

'Damnation. OK, everyone, we're gonna comb those woods and get those sonsabitches.'

The men at the barricade were mounting up. Marshal Howarth held up his hand for attention.

'Spread out along the road,' he yelled. 'We'll make a sweep through the trees. Keep in a line if you can. I want them varmints caught. But don't put yourself in danger. If there's any doubt they ain't gonna surrender – shoot. Don't take any chances. All right men, move out.'

Verne Lecroy accompanied by Tex Plant rode into the trees behind the posse.

'I wanna be there when they corner those curly wolves,' Lecroy growled. 'There's someone with them I need to settle scores with. Blackwell said Blain Larkin is with them. He escaped justice once, but looks like this is a chance to put that right. We follow those lawmen. Let them corral the varmints and we'll move in and finish them. I wanna be the one to kill that son of a bitch Larkin. You heard the marshal. He wants to bring them in for a hanging. We tried that once before, and the slippery lizard got away. Well, not this time. A bullet in the head is a sure-fire way of making certain justice is done.'

'Don't worry, boss. I'll make sure you're in at the kill,' Tex Plant assured him.

As the outlaws fled through the trees, Blain's horse stepped in a hole. Blain heard the leg break even as he went over its head. He rolled with the fall and came up winded but otherwise uninjured. The horse grunted in pain and tried to stand on the broken limb. Blain crawled to the horse and pulled his rifle from the scabbard. Though he knew it would give away his position he could not bear to see it suffer. He put the muzzle of the rifle against its skull and pulled the trigger. It was a clean shot and the horse collapsed in the dirt.

Blain heard shouting and ran further into the woods. He heard a rider approaching and waited, pressed up against an oak tree, the thick trunk providing cover. He held his rifle at the ready. A deputy went trotting past, too busy watching for low branches to notice the youngster. Blain waited until the rider was past and decided to reload the Remington he had emptied at the ambushers back at the railhead. Once he had fully loaded the gun, he stuck it back in his belt.

All around him Blain could hear shouting and the noise of horses crashing through the trees. He decided to stop where he was for the moment and await developments. Then a horse brushed against the tree that was sheltering him, and the deputy spotted him. The rider cursed and swung his revolver towards the crouching youngster.

Blain lashed out with his rifle as the lawman pulled the trigger. The bullet went somewhere into the undergrowth. The startled horse skittered sideways and the rider, off balance, grabbed for the saddle horn. Blain fired at the cursing deputy, the shot hitting him in the side of the head. He lost his seat as the panicked animal reared. It was Blain who was cursing now as he made a wild grab for the bridle but the horse swerved to one side and bolted.

'Damn and blast!'

A tremendous blow struck Blain's rifle as a bullet hit it, and the gun was jarred from his hands. He looked up and saw another deputy firing at him. The lawman's horse, unnerved by the shooting going on amongst the trees, was jumping around and caused the shot to miss. Desperately Blain flung himself behind the tree.

He twisted awkwardly away, losing sight of the man for the moment. Then he saw him again. His mouth was open in a scream of agony as a bullet hit him in the stomach. Blain caught sight of a grimfaced Wilbur Borgman as he turned to face another of the enemy. The horse kept running, and Blain couldn't see if Borgman had managed to hit him.

Quickly Blain bent and retrieved his broken rifle. There came a crashing from his left. He swung round to face this new danger, and the horse was upon him before he could take evasive action.

It was like being hit with an anvil, and Blain was knocked clean off his feet. The man on top of the horse was snarling as he fired at the youth. Even as he was falling, Blain swung with his useless rife. He managed to hit the rider's leg and then the horse carried him past. Blain could hear the man cursing as he reined in the horse.

The bushes slowed the horse and the rider was regaining control and was coming back on the attack again.

34

Blain looked up and the horseman had managed to turn his mount and was advancing towards him. Dazedly he struggled to retain his feet, using his rifle as a prop to push himself erect.

The horseman was cursing and pushing the horse through the bushes. Blain stared with consternation. He blinked and blinked again. For a moment he was back in another time – his brother lying dead with a treacherous bullet in him.

'Lecroy!' he yelled. 'Lecroy, you killed my brother. Now I'm gonna kill you.'

With a shock Verne realized who his opponent was.

'Larkin!'

Verne was walking his horse towards Blain. He aimed his gun and pulled the trigger. All that happened was a click. Lecroy looked askance at the weapon and swiftly pouched it. He pulled a knife and held it up whilst leering at his victim.

'There's a price on your head, Larkin. I guess I'll take that head back to my pa.'

Blain was staring with intense bitterness at the horseman. All his woes stemmed from this one man and his wanton act of murder. Now with some peculiar twist of fate they were face to face in a wood. One thing was clear. Only one of them would survive this encounter.

'A sprat like you won't take much killing.' Lecroy snarled.

'They'll have to bury you without your head, for I'm taking that back with me. Pa will probably make it into a spittoon.' Verne threw back his head and laughed. 'What a joke that'll be; to spit in your head. It'll not be much different as to what's in there at present.'

Blain was regaining his second wind. He was also bolstered by the hatred seething through his blood at the sight of his old enemy. Gripping his useless rifle in both hands he was watching closely the movements of the horseman moving in on him.

Verne was fast. If the sweep with his knife had landed, his boast of taking Blain's head back would have been accomplished. Blain was almost caught napping. He flung himself back and parried the blade with his rifle.

Lecroy was suddenly anxious to finish this encounter. He urged his horse towards Blain slashing wildly at him with the knife. Blain was at a disadvantage, for he was on the ground and trying to strike his enemy who was mounted above him. Verne was in possession of two weapons. As well as his knife he was wielding, he was pushing his horse at Blain, using it as a battering ram. Blain was forced to retreat while at the same time keeping out of the range of that deadly blade.

Time seemed suspended as Blain fought. Once more he was back in a different world with the dead body of his brother lying in the dirt. That same killing rage was upon him.

He kept going back, watching that shining blade slashing through the air at him. Again and again he parried as the man on the horse pushed him further and further. Blain's arms were growing tired under the constant hefting of his rifle. The pain in his chest where the horse had struck was intensifying. Desperately he fought on, seeking an opportunity to strike his enemy with his rifle.

The clash of steel rang out as he fought the duel with

Lecroy. Then disaster struck. As Blain went backwards, his heel caught on a projecting root. The youngster tumbled onto his back. The horse loomed over him. He could see the triumphant face of his enemy leering down at him. Lecroy was swinging the blade towards the youngster.

Blain thrust desperately up at the rider in a frantic effort at self-preservation. Lecroy smashed his blade down against the weapon in an effort to knock it from Blain's grasp. He did not succeed, but he did deflect the gun and turn it beneath his mount.

The steel muzzle jabbed into soft flesh. The horse arched its neck and let out a high-pitched whinny. It whirled and jerked away from the thing biting into its throat, its hoofs smashing down on the earth as it plunged in panic. Blain had to roll frantically to escape injury from those iron-shod hoofs.

Lecroy had to give his whole effort to staying in the saddle. The horse bucked and thrashed around. In open country Lecroy would probably have managed to stay aboard. As it was, the low-hanging branches in the thick of the wood were his undoing, and with a yell of terror he was unseated. Coming down heavily, his head hit the trunk of a tree and he collapsed, dazed and winded.

Blain was back on his feet. Hardly believing his deliverance, he staggered over to the fallen man. He stood over Lecroy lying in the dirt.

'Die, you murdering bastard! This is for Moylan.'

He raised the rifle, ready to club his enemy, and then hesitated. He had killed in the heat of fighting, but to do so now in cold blood? They had fought and he had won. Had the situation been reversed, Blain had no doubt Lecroy would not have hesitated to plunge his knife into Blain's heart. He stared down at Lecroy, and still he could not do the deed.

'Please. . . .'

Lecroy was staring up at Blain with pleading eyes.

147

'Don't kill me . . . please.'

'Blain! Blain!'

The voice called urgently, and Blain recognized it as Robert's. He backed away from the helpless man on the ground.

'Here, over here.'

Robert pushed through the undergrowth.

'Thank God I found you. I feared the worst. Wilbur Borgman said he saw you over in this direction.' Sturdy caught sight of Lecroy. 'What's this?'

'This is Verne Lecroy, the man who murdered my brother and then had me tried for murder. I know I should kill him, but I don't know if I can.'

'Do you want me to do the deed?' Sturdy asked, pulling his Colt.

As he spoke he stepped in between Blain and Lecroy – and at that moment a shot rang out and a hole appeared in his chest. As Robert pitched forwards, Blain felt something punch him in the shoulder. The bullet that had killed Sturdy had passed right through his body and wounded him as well. Both men went down with Blain underneath, the gang leader's eyes wide and staring at him.

35

'Mr Lecroy, are you OK?'

Tex Plant came forward, a smoking pistol in his hand. Lecroy was staring with disbelief at the bodies sprawled beside him.

'Plant, thank God you came when you did. These bastards were about to murder me.'

Blain lay beneath Robert, feeling the wetness soaking from the bullet wound in his arm. There was pain also, but worse than that was the sight of Robert with wide vacant eyes lying on top of him.

I have killed her brother, he thought. But I shall die with him.

The dead man was a solid weight, pressing down on him, crushing him into the dirt.

'Make sure the bastards are dead.'

'Sure thing boss – I saw your horse running loose and came looking for you. Good job I did.'

There was a grunt, and Blain felt the weight of Robert's body lifted from him.

'This one's dead, anyway.'

Blain almost screamed aloud as a hand grabbed his injured shoulder. He opened his eyes and stared up at the face of Tex Plant.

'This other fella's still alive. Shall I finish him?'

'No, I want to do it. I have a score to settle with that one.'

Lecroy loomed up in Blain's vision.

'Take that damned rifle away from him. He hurt my horse with that thing.'

The rifle was pulled from Blain's grasp. He let his hand fall limply across his waist and encountered the Remington stuffed in his belt. Lecroy stood leering at him, the knife in his hand.

'Blain Larkin, in the name of justice, I sentence you to death by beheading.'

Blain pulled the Remington. He was fumbling to cock it with one hand. His other hand was lying numb and useless by his side. Lecroy's eyes went wide with shock. The gun bucked in Blain's hand. The bullet entered below Lecroy's chin and went out through the top of his head. Lecroy stepped back, his mouth and eyes wide as his head exploded. Then he went down like a felled tree, dropping neatly beside Blain. Hot blood splashed on Blain's face as the corpse thudded down beside him.

Tex Plant, as much taken by surprise as his boss, was standing to one side holding Blain's rifle. With quick thinking he drove the weapon down at the wounded youth. Blain screamed as the butt hit him on his wounded shoulder. Plant flung himself on top of him, knocking the Remington from his hand. Blain felt fingers like iron bands grip his throat.

'You've killed Lecroy, you bastard. Die! Die! Die!'

The man jerked hard on Blain's neck, lifting him up and thumping his head back against the earth. With his wounded arm dangling helplessly, Blain could only scrabble ineffectually with one hand at the rigid bands encircling his neck.

Blain's eyes bulged and his face became mottled. He stared up at the contused face of the man on top of him. Feebly he twisted under the big man's weight. There was no give in the rigidity of his attacker: it was as if he were built from oak.

Above Plant's head Blain noticed the branches and leaves of the trees. Through the foliage he could see patches of blue sky and the bright sunlight. His hand fell limply away.

In his agony his fingers dug into the dirt, scoring deep lines. His groping encountered something metallic. Strangely detached, he explored the object. Even as he groped at it, the world was dimming. There was fire in his lungs. He was staring up at the leaves above his head – but his hand curled around the hilt of Lecroy's knife.

'Die!' Plant gritted out through clenched teeth.

Spittle dripped on Blain's face – but his hand was gripping the hilt of the knife, raising it. From the corner of his blurry, blood-tinted vision he could see the blade. A shaft of sunlight peeped through the leaf cover, glinting on the shiny steel.

Plant sensed something and turned his head. With his last desperate strength, Blain shoved the knife hard into his assailant's neck, the steel going in underneath Plant's ear. With all his draining strength Blain rammed the blade deeper and deeper.

Plant's mouth was open and blood was gushing from his lips. His fingers lifted from Blain's neck. The gunman clutched at the knife, his hands slippery with the blood from the wound. The knife was jammed up inside his head, grating on bone. He fell to one side, on top of the dead Lecroy. Plant's mouth gaped open, emitting ghastly strangulated noises as he struggled to free the blade. His legs kicked wildly in his agony.

Beside the dying man, Blain tried to rise, to get away from the gruesome contortions taking place beside him, but the effort was too much. He collapsed back to the earth, his throat raw as he sucked in life-giving air, his shoulder on fire where the bullet that had killed Robert Sturdy had entered. Lying amongst the dead and dying, Blain gave up the struggle – he closed his eyes and drifted off into a dark and cavernous place.

36

'Larkin.' A voice was grating in his ear. 'I've come to kill you, Larkin. Wake up. I want you to watch while I finish you.'

Blain knew it was part of the nightmare. One by one the corpses reared up, showing him their gaping wounds. Lecroy lurched over to him and twisted his head round so Blain could view the back of his ruined skull.

'I'll come for you, Larkin. One night when you least expect, I'll come and tell you what it's like in hell.'

Beside Lecroy, the man who had shot Sturdy sat up. He leered at Blain.

'We have you now, Larkin.'

The words were slurred and bubbling, coming out mixed with gouts of blood.

Robert's face deadly pale.

'You killed me, Blain! I never wanted to die.'

Maggots crawled from Robert's mouth as he spoke. He was lying in the dirt, staring up at Blain, his body splattered with blood.

There was the dull insistent pounding on his shoulder and the agony of it pulling him back up to the surface. It was dim in the room. He peered at the shadowy figure looming over him. The man was holding something in his hand and hitting Blain's bandaged shoulder with it.

'Larkin, are you awake? Can you hear me?'

Blain stared up at the face of the man hovering over him. Slowly his senses began to function. His first sensation was one of pain. His upper body was a harsh zone of hurting.

'Where am I?' he croaked.

'Back at the hideout. Your buddy Jephta brought you in.'

Blain was floating in a sea of pain. Memory was coming back. The fight in the wood. Robert lying across him, staring accusingly with those sightless eyes. Suddenly it was too much. Blain groaned.

'No, I couldn't help it. It should have been me, not you!'

As the pain grew, a dark mist crept across his brain and he was drifting back down again into that black pit. Then his shoulder agony as something hard pounded it.

'Wake up, Larkin. This is no time for sleeping.'

'Whaa . . .' he moaned, 'stop hitting me.'

The object that had been drumming so painfully on his wound was moved to his face. He could see the shine of a knife blade.

'Just leave me alone.'

'Hah! That's just what we won't do. We've come to settle a debt.'

Blain was beginning to think that perhaps this was not part of his nightmare. He struggled to make out the man crouching over him.

'What is it? What do you want?'

A match flared and Blain stared at the craggy features of Blackwell. On the other side of his bunk another figure came into view. He knew instinctively it could only be Willer.

'We been searching for you, Larkin. I looked for you during the fighting, but you were hiding somewhere like a frightened rat. You should have died out there, Larkin. Somehow you got away. Now I've come to finish you.'

As Blackwell stopped speaking the match flickered and went out. Blain was left with the image of the outlaw's creased and ugly face.

'You hear me, Larkin. We're here to kill you.'

He could just make out the blade in front of his face. Blackwell drew it down along Blain's cheek just hard enough to break the skin and draw blood.

'You see, we'll cut you up some so as you bleed to death. Maybe I'll help bury you.'

Willer sniggered.

'Me too. I want to shovel dirt on that son of a bitch.'

Blain stared up into Blackwell's features that he could barely see – and suddenly the thing he had wanted was about to happen: it seemed that from this unlikely quarter he was to get his wish and die. The ghosts would cease to haunt him. He would join them.

'Cut,' he said. 'Cut and be damned to you!'

He could feel Blackwell pulling back his blanket. He stared up into the rafters in the ceiling and waited for the blade.

'I'm gonna stick it in your gut. Make a nice big hole. You'll just bleed to death. It'll be slow and painful. Enjoy.'

Blain felt strangely detached as he watched the knife rise in the air. His time had come. He had endured so much. It was time for it all to end.

37

Willer gave a low-key grunted warning. Blackwell paused, his knife poised above the youngster in the bed. Willer was staring at something beyond Blackwell. Blackwell was turning – but he never quite made that turn, and he never knew what it was that hit him. The axe smashed into the side of his head, cutting off a portion of his ear and breaking open his skull. He slithered to the floor, blood and brains spilling.

Willer turned to run, tripped and went down. As he was scrambling on all fours to get away, the axe struck again. The heavy blade buried itself in the back of his head. It split like a melon, and Willer died instantly, without a sound.

'Blain, are you all right?'

'Jephta, is that you Jephta?'

'Sure thing, looks like I came by in the nick of time. I saw them pair prowling about up here. Knew they were up to no good.'

'You kill 'em both?'

'Dead as lice on a hot knife. I'll drag 'em outside.'

Blain waited as Jephta lugged first Blackwell and then Willer from the room, leaving dark streaks across the floor. When Jephta returned, he leaned over Blain.

'What happened back in that wood? I never saw you again until I found you and Robert and a couple of other galoots. Looks like a helluva fight you and Sturdy put up. I thought you were dead.'

'It was Lecroy. Robert offered to kill him for me.'

'Lecroy! You mean the fella as killed your brother.'

'He was the cause of all my troubles. He's dead now and rotting in hell along with the viper that shot Sturdy.'

'You killed them both!'

'I shot Lecroy. Blew his damn head apart. I killed the other fella with a knife.'

'Goddamn it, Blain, I'm proud of you.'

'Jephta, how many died out there?'

'Hell I know! I was just shooting and running. Weren't no time to keep tally. I was just glad to get outta there alive. We lost a lotta good men.'

'Did it bother you? All that killing?'

'Didn't feel nothin', killing 'em. Same as I felt nothing killing those two scum, Blackwell and Willer. You survive by killing fellas as is trying to kill you. I don't think about it – I just do it.'

'I guess.'

Jephta fumbled in his tunic.

'With all this going on I almost forgot. I gotta letter for you.'

Jephta held up an envelope.

'A letter! Who'd be writing to me? Ain't no one knows where I'm at.'

In the dim light Blain could just make out the rectangle shape of the letter. He reached out and took it. There was the faint smell of flowers from the paper. It reminded him of someone, but he dismissed it instantly.

'Are you sure it's addressed to me?'

'Yep, there's one for Robert, too.'

Blain felt the lump in his throat. For a time he did not speak.

'Jephta, I gotta read this letter. Can you find a light somewhere?'

'Sure thing.'

When Jephta returned with a lamp, Blain had managed to hitch himself higher on the pillow. In the dim light he peered at the envelope.

'It is addressed to me. I have a feeling I know who it might be. I'm afraid to read it.'

'Here, give it to me.' Jephta held his hand out. 'I'll set it on fire and you won't need to read it.'

'Damn you, Jephta, you'll do no such thing.'

Jephta chuckled.

'I didn't think you'd allow it.'

'Open it for me. The arm's not so good.'

There was a single sheet covered in a fine, even script. Quickly Blain scanned the signature.

'Miss Emelie Sturdy,' he whispered.

Jephta squeezed on the bunk beside Blain and held the lamp so the light fell on the paper. There was silence as Blain read silently.

Dear Mr Blain Larkin,

I did not want to write this letter but something inside me obliged me. That awful night is still with me. Balanced against that is the precious time we had together. Robert came to me before he left and told me not to be hard on you. When he was gone, I suddenly had this rare insight. I had felt so self-righteous and condemned you without knowing anything about you or that woman. I looked at myself in the mirror and imagined I was just like my father, so stern and unbending. It upset me not a little.

I have written to Robert telling him he is to bring you back on his next visit. If you so wish you can call upon me. I have told Father. He strongly disapproves but I told him I must give you a chance to explain.

Perhaps if I have the courage I will call upon that woman who behaved so with you.

Come back safely. You and Robert and Jephta. May God preserve you all. I am praying very hard for you.

Miss Emelie Sturdy.

There was a lump in Blain's throat as big as a turkey egg.

'What she say?' Jephta asked.

Blain couldn't speak. He handed the paper over. Jephta did not take it, but sat there, not looking at the letter. Blain shook the paper impatiently.

'Ain't no use, Blain. I can't read.'

'Sorry Jephta, I didn't know.'

They were silent then, wrapped in their own private thoughts. Blain gave a long sigh that came from somewhere deep inside.

'Emelie doesn't know Robert is dead. She's written him a letter. Wants him to bring me with him when next he visits.'

The last few words came out as a sob.

'Oh damn! Oh damn and blast!' Jephta swore.

'I'll have to go and see her; tell her about Robert. You'll come with me, won't you Jephta?'

A hand rested on Blain's shoulder.

'I sure will.'

A long silence fell between them. Jephta sat quietly. In time he heard a curious snuffling noise. He held up the lantern

157

and peered at his friend. Blain Larkin was fast asleep. Clutched in his hand was the envelope that carried with it the faint aroma of flowers.